CW01080510

# ⌐
# BLACKWATERFOOT

## MILLER CALDWELL

# BeulAithris
## Publishing

Scotland

www.beul-aithris-publishing.com

First edition 2021

ISBN: 9798745215872

© Miller Caldwell 2021

No copying of the material within allowed
without the express permission of the author and
publisher, apart from under fair use

*This novel's story and characters are fictitious. Certain long-standing institutions, agencies and public offices are also mentioned, and the characters involved are wholly imaginary.*

# ABOUT THE AUTHOR

Miller Caldwell is a Scottish based writer of novels, biographies, self-help and children's books. He holds a post-graduate degree from London University. He has had articles published in health magazines and The Scottish Review.

In a life of humanitarian work in Ghana, Pakistan and Scotland, he has gained remarkable insights into human nature through confronting Osama bin Laden near Abbottabad in 2006 and bringing an African President to tears in West Africa in 2002. He was the local chair of the Scottish Association for the Study of Offending for twelve years. He served on the committee of the Society of Authors in Scotland and was its events manager.

Miller plays a variety of brass, woodwind and keyboard instruments. They provide a break from writing. Married, he has two daughters and he lives in Dumfries.

www.millercaldwell.com

# ACKNOWLEDGEMENTS

Thank you, Arran and the bull, you inspired the book. Many thanks too, to the Detective Constable, who clarified timescales and advised me of criminal procedure. I am unable to mention her by name. Thanks to Jen and her dog Rubik for permission to appear. David Watt in France came to my rescue before publication with his eagle eye and sharp pencil. Merci beacoup. Vous êtes sans pairs et un editeur merveilleux. To M J Steel Collins my editor and publisher, I am truly grateful. I'm in very good hands.

Finally to my wife, Jocelyn, who gives me enough time to daydream, plot and write. And of course, to our collie Georgie, who enjoys her holidays on Arran and insists on three walks a day on the banks of the river Nith at Dumfries.

*Dedicated to Joan and Ian Young*

# 1

Constable Rory Murdoch knew he was the luckiest policeman in Scotland. Nothing of importance ever occurred on his rural island beat. He was born on Arran, went to school there, and apart from his police training at the Tulliallan Police College in the Central Belt of Scotland, his life had been spent on the jewel of the Clyde which is the peaceful and sedate island of Arran. He was popular and very well known as his duty car leisurely circled the rugby ball-shaped isle. He had no enemies. *Why create angst* seemed to be his motto. Vehicle collisions, more often than not with a farm trailer, were among the occasional noteworthy incidents and the rowdy evening drinkers at the weekend formed the rest of his logbook, which rarely saw him turn a page in a month. Even Friday night brawls were humanely resolved with Rory's friendly pat on the back or the occasional kick on the backside, telling the offenders not to be so silly and get home to their beds. They usually took his advice, so the Sheriff had little to do which suited his leisurely golfing requirements over the entire island's seven links courses and defence lawyers concentrated on house sales, they being a more lucrative business.

Rory was based at the Lamlash police station on the east side of the island, in a residential part of the town where confident crows roosting nearby, created a noisy holler especially after bursts of rain.

The phone rang just when he was pouring his favourite Guatemalan coffee into his Police Scotland blue-diced mug. He stirred two spoonfuls of sugar into his drink before sipping it. Then he lifted the phone.

'Constable Murdoch here, how can I help you?' he said with his usual friendly opening remark. He listened intently while his other hand disturbed some official and some not so official papers, searching for his pen and pad.

'Now, what you are telling me, er .... Mr....'

'John Maxwell.'

'Mr. Maxwell, yes, is that you have found a body. Is that right?' His writing pad was ready to receive the urgent and surprisingly unusual information he was receiving that dull morning.

'And where is the body, sir.... I see, at the bottom of the garden, yes?'

The caller spoke in short breaths in a fast manner, clearly flabbergasted at his discovery, and gave the impression he had never been in this macabre situation before. Neither had Rory. The deceased was in a field at the bottom of the garden of the house Mr. Maxwell had rented for the week. The exact location was about a mile south of Blackwaterfoot, at Kilpatrick, he told Rory.

There was a hesitation. Murdoch had to think quickly. He had only come across a murder in training. He was definitely out of his depth.

'I'll be round soon. Er...don't touch the body and don't let anyone else get near it,' he said with authority. 'Oh and.... you are really sure the body is deceased?'

'Very much so. It's certainly not a recent crime, I'm sure of that.'

An uncontrolled shudder travelled through Rory's body. He replaced the phone, still holding it down in its cradle to steady himself and his thoughts.

Then he lifted his coffee and ate a Glengarry biscuit. His morning elevenses were sacrosanct, providing good thinking time. Usually, that time was for him to complete his Daily Record crossword puzzle but on this occasion, the word 'murder' was the six-letter word at the fore of his thoughts and that word did not fit into any of the blank squares.

# 2

As Rory set off from Lamlash, with his fingers drumming on his steering wheel, he wondered who might have come to such a tragic end and, of course, who could have committed the crime. He tried to recall his school contemporaries who were still on that part of the island. None stood out capable of such a deed. Of course, there had been many incomers over recent years. There were the octogenarians wishing to end their days in the fresh sea air. Younger families setting out on artistic pursuits and ensuring schooling was neither crowded nor urban. He assumed it could not be one of his acquaintances. They simply didn't do murder, surely? The elderly? Unlikely. The rest? A missing person would certainly have been reported. He shook his head bewildered and unsure where to start this murder enquiry.

He approached the sleepy hamlet of Kilpatrick, with Blackwaterfoot visible in the near distance. A few white-walled farmhouses sat in the glistening sun on the hill above the main road. A view of splattered sheep looked like large daisies to Rory as they entered his line of vision.

The deluge of rain that had battered the island over the past ten days had subsided. Blue skies and sharp sunshine replaced the recent gloom but the ground was as soft as moss and the well-maintained roads were still wet. There was a string of dispersed cottages along the road. He slowed the car down and strained his eyes to read the names of the homes.

Auchenbarry Cottage came into view. A man appeared at the front door. Rory had reached the scene of the crime. He parked at the side of the white guest house.

John was around forty-five years of age or so. He wore a rusty red jumper with cream trousers and his hands lay on top of his hips. His accent was possibly East Coast but whether Edinburgh or Fife, Rory could not be sure.

'Constable Murdoch?' he enquired unnecessarily. 'I'm John, John Maxwell. It was me who found the body.'

'Can you take me there?' Rory asked as he locked the police car door.

'Yes, come this way. Actually, I didn't really find the body. You see it's been very wet recently as you know. My collie, Georgie, was barking. That's what made me wonder what she was seeing. It seems the bull in the field over the hedge had been.... well, scratching at a mound with its hoof and the body appeared. It seems as simple as that.'

'A bull uncovering a body? Most unusual, I'd say,' said Rory Murdoch striding down the lawn.

'Oh, it did not uncover the whole body. It's just a hand I found. I presume there's a body underground,' he said scratching his head.

PC Murdoch peered over the thorn hedge. He tipped his police cap back as he did so. Perhaps it was not a corpse after all. Then he focussed on the mound of grass. Sure enough, the field had been disturbed by the bull and a skeletal bony hand, no more than that, was visible.

He stroked his chin four times. Then he took out his mobile phone and called his superior on the Ayrshire mainland.

'It's only a hand at this stage I've seen.... Yes, Sir, in the ground.......Okay and a forensic team too? Great.'

He gave his superior colleague the exact location. They would arrive half an hour after the boat landed at Brodick. It should take them less than twenty-five minutes to cross over the island on the B road to the scene. Two of the island's four police cars would bring them to the body.

Rory forced his way through the hedge at the end of the garden and produced some police marking tape. He laid it on the ground and secured it with six heavy stones taken from the nearby stream.

Rory bent down and studied the exposed hand. It was clearly a hand that had been in the ground for some time. It was no longer wrinkled or ashen grey but a hand of mainly skeletal bones. He deduced the body had indeed been there for ages. Perhaps a woman's hand, the delicacy of the bones, he thought. Yet it was so decayed it was difficult to glean any more facts.

'Well, that's all we can do for the time being. I've called for a forensic team to do their work,' he said sounding unusually official in his delivery.

'Then, can I invite you in for a coffee?'

Rory looked around. The only sound he heard was the rippling waves over a pebbly beach some two hundred yards away. Typical of the west coast of Arran was its solitude, its deserted beaches and sun-drenched rocks supporting lazy basking seals. It was restful. This field perhaps was an ideal place to bury a body.

'Coffee yes, that's a good idea, John.'

'Nice house you've found here,' Rory said to John's slim wife in tartan jeans and a matching lovat-green jumper. 'Yes, we like it here. It's our second year at Achnabarry. We don't usually come back to the same guest house but the September break last year was such a great retreat from the city, we decided to return.'

Their collie sniffed Constable Murdoch's trousers and then his groin. Rory placed his hand on its head and gave it a friendly shake.

'Nice dog you have, clever too.'

'That's what they say about collies, loyal and clever,' she said. Rory nodded as the water in the kettle reached boiling point before switching off.

'So, you are both from Edinburgh?' he enquired.

Yes, sorry I should have said, I'm Morag, John's wife,' she declared as she lined up the mugs and dropped a spoonful of granulated coffee into each.

'Viewforth Terrace, not far from the city centre. Sugar and milk?'

'Yes both, two spoonfuls of sugar, thanks,' replied Rory unable to identify that specific part of Edinburgh.

John sauntered through to the kitchen to join them. 'So, not many murders on Arran?'

'Tourists come for holidays and the residents seem to know each other. Not much scope for murder on any island. Of course, there was a famous Goat Fell murder but that was a couple of generations ago.'

'Yes, the Goat Fell Murder. 1889 I think. Quite a famous case too,' John recalled.

'Yup you got your dates right. So you know about murders?' Rory asked tilting his head towards John.

'Mainly through detective books. Denise Mina, Ian Rankin, Lee Child, John Grisham, those sorts of murders,' John smiled and sat back on the ladder-backed wooden chair wondering if he had implied he knew too much about murder.

Rory pouted his lips and nodded. 'You seem to like murders better than me.'

'Relaxation for me, work for you,' John said sipping his hot coffee and peering over his mug to gauge Rory's reaction to his apparent profound comment.

**3**

Two and a half hours later, as clouds started to congregate once more, two police cars drew up at Auchenbarry Cottage and parked on the green verge by the road. Detective Inspector Sammy Grant switched off the engine and emerged into the cool late afternoon. He filled his lungs in the sea air while observing the white-walled extended property. He wore a smart grey suit with shoes so black and shiny they looked as if they had come directly from the dance floor. From the other door appeared a woman in jeans and a heavy sky-blue jumper. Her bulky anorak had a Val d'Isère logo on her back. She was in her mid-thirties with no wedding ring on her finger. Her shoes were practical, brown, and flat-heeled. She greeted Rory.

'Constable Murdoch,' she said offering her hand. 'I'm Dr. Jane Dunbar, forensic scientist.'

Rory nodded. 'Good, I'm sure you will move the case on.'

From the other car emerged two police officers in their number twos. They were wearing heavy boots and dark uniform work clothes. They carried spades and a canvass screen.

'Exhume, and then move the body to the mortuary at Brodick,' said D.I. Grant in an officious tone.

'Won't you want to examine the immediate vicinity first?' asked Rory.

D.I. Grant drew his eyebrows together and stared at Rory. 'Of course, but I expected you would have done that by now.'

Rory felt the pang of a reprimand. His repost was quick. 'Short staffed on the island. No one to corroborate any inspection sir,' said Rory standing tall with an air of "you're not so smart," about him.

'Let's see the body then,' growled the Inspector showing Rory little respect.

Rory led him down the garden to the compost pit from where there was access to the field.

'Good to see the police tape in position,' said D.I. Grant,' in a subdued voice.

'Almost unnecessary,' suggested Rory. 'No one knows about the body. We're in the middle of nowhere here,' he said proud to have the chance to share Arran's special solitude.

'Utter nonsense. The mainland knows about the murder and they will have an Arran journalist here before long to get some facts about the case.'

Rory nodded with pouted lips. These Police Scotland mainlanders must have the press at their door. It simply was not the Lamlash way of doing things. Rory always phoned the journalists at the Arran Banner if he had a story to tell.

As Rory turned round, he glanced at Morag and John standing by the lounge bay-window. John stood behind his wife with his hands on her shoulders. They looked anxious and unwilling to miss any of the developments at their holiday home.

# 4

Carefully the spades laid bare more of the skeleton. It seemed to be a small victim, perhaps even a child. By the time the pelvic bones appeared, Jane knew this had been the body of a dainty mature woman. She placed a sizeable chip of bone into a tube. DNA might be able to identify who the deceased was and possibly who had caused her death. There were no rings, clothing, or any jewellery to assist further identification.

'Rory, give me your book of missing Arran people. Take it back a few years. There can't be many,' instructed D.I. Sammy Grant.

Rory thought where the book might be. He drew a blank but did not wish to inform his superior. 'Yes, I'll do that when I get back to Lamlash,' he said. 'Will you do a full Scottish trawl of missing people as well?'

The D.I. turned to Rory. 'Let's take our time. Eliminate the locals first. If nothing comes up, it will be much harder. Yes, there will be a wider check. There's no rush. The murder was not last night.'

On his way back to the office Rory gave thought to his filing cabinet. Yes, there was a 'missing' folder. It was actually a missing/lost folder because missing keys were reported, then a few hours later the caller would report they had been found. Missing dogs too. They usually returned home at their leisure. Missing persons? No, he did not have one. Perhaps he had better start a new file.

An hour or so after his return to the station, as his crossword's last box was about to be filled, the telephone rang.

'Ah Jane, yes, any progress?'

'We've moved the body to Brodick and I've made an initial assessment. The body has been in the ground for about a year. 12-18 months I reckon. No more; no less. I suppose that doesn't give you a great start,' she said as her voice drained away.

'That holiday cottage, it's been there a long time. Perhaps it is worth investigating again,' said Rory giving what he thought might be a plausible next step.

'Yes, that's a good idea. I'll leave that in your capable hands,' said Jane

'Yes, okay. But keep me updated if you can,' he responded, winding the telephone cord around his fingers.

'Certainly, I'd love to return to Arran.'

'You mean you are leaving us?' asked Rory, his voice rising as he spoke.

'Yes, a DNA matching in Glasgow is called for now. I'll see what that digs up.'

Rory grinned. A wider mainland search was underway after all.

With a body over a year old and nobody reported as a missing person, Rory settled down to his perambulations around Lamlash, his outings to Lochranza in the north of the island and his shoreline walks with his Springer spaniel, Flop. It was those elongated drooping ears that named his dog. Rory was an almost practical man. He had to be. His domestic life was demanding. His wife died giving birth to his premature daughter, Ella. She was his life and his devotion to her and her needs were total.

As the trees turned golden brown and a nip in the air met Rory's early morning patrols, Detective Inspector Sammy Grant gave him a call.

'Presumably nothing to go on yet in that murder?' he asked.

Rory shook his head. 'Nothing at all, except the forensic girl. Jane said the body in the ground is about a year old.' Rory could hear his boss breathing the silence, thinking.

'Was there not a visitor's book in the cottage?'

'A visitor's book? Well, I suppose so. Very likely I would think.'

'Then get your fat arse over there and get hold of it. Oh, better inform the owner that you are taking it away as well.'

'Yes Sir, right away,' said Rory eyeing his kettle. As he poured his coffee, he thought what an uncompromising boss he had in the foul-mouthed D.I. Grant.

The cottage was owned by a lady who lived in Aberdeen. In his notes of the murder taken at the cottage, he had recorded the owner's details. He rang Karla Hodge.

'Mrs. Hodge, PC Rory Murdoch here in Lamlash, I hope you are well?' he asked in his polite manner.

'Um, yes I am fine. Have you got the murderer? I've heard about it on the BBC radio link. You know the i-thingy?'

'Er...no we are not at that stage yet. In fact, it will take some time. I'm ringing you to take your visitors' book at the cottage into my possession, if I may.'

Karla hesitated. 'You mean it was a guest of mine who murdered the woman?' she said raising her voice an octave.

'We are keeping an open mind about it,' Rory reassured her.

'But you must have some reason to take the book, surely? I mean it will list all my guests.'

'It will be a list to eliminate each of them. That's all we are doing, honestly. We may have to come back to you for some personality checks perhaps, but don't be alarmed.'

'A personality check?' she asked. 'I book them by e-mail and phone. I never see any of them.'

'Oh,' thought Rory. 'Then we might not have to contact you after all. But I have your permission? The visitor's book?'

'Of course, if you must. And it will be returned, I presume.'

'It certainly will, I assure you,' Rory said in an official tone.

'Then you'll get a key for the cottage from the next-door neighbour if the holidaymakers are not in. Please do not upset them, if they are.'

'Discretion is part of my training,' said Rory ending the call. Then he let out a deep sigh. Karla Hodge had been no pushover.

The day's work had concluded at the office. Rory stopped on his way home at the Brodick Co-op and filled his trolley. He had made a list while eating his Cheerios over breakfast that morning but as usual, his eye always found a bargain or a treat making it a surprise when he got home to his daughter. Eggs, milk, and sausages were on the list but he filled his trolley to the full. The calming effect of the rubber-running trolley wheels kept work from dominating his thoughts. But he was still in uniform.

'Got the killer yet, constable?' asked a man of around forty years of age and looking like a former rugby prop with an attitude.

'Working on it, I assure you,' he said with a smile feeling this man could turn out to be the murderer perhaps, one day.

'Can I sleep soundly?' asked an elderly woman with a congested frown and a wheezy chest.

Rory patted her shoulder. 'Sleep like a log. The killer is probably on the mainland.'

She smiled at his reassuring words but also in the knowledge of the demands his work required.

Rory staggered out of the car at home with his provisions, to hear Flop barking inside the house.

He placed his bags down and his key engaged the lock. The door opened and Flop emerged undecided whether to give master his welcoming attention or to concentrate on the food now at nose level.

The wheelchair came slowly along the hallway and stopped. Ella thrust out her arms and welcomed her father home. He clung on to her despite the growing pain his bending back felt.

'Toad-in-the hole, tonight. Okay?'

Ella's joy was confirmed in a smile and a giggle.

Rory wheeled Ella through to the lounge. He switched on the television.

'We've missed the start. It's the second round of Pointless. Is that all right for you?'

'Yes Dad,' she said still smiling at her father. She spun her chair round the settee and rested with the brake applied in front of the screen.

'Oh that's 100, no not Prime Minister Gordon Douglas-Home,' said Xander, the Pointless host.

'I'll give the correct answers at the end of the round,' said Richard in a sympathetic voice hiding a grin at the answer given.

'Okay, shout me through for the news. I'll start the cooking,' said her father as he entered the kitchen.

# 5

Rory sat down in the lounge of the holiday home and flipped through the pages of the visitor's book in a casual manner. From time to time he looked out through the front picture window to the hedge beyond, where the body had been found. All he could see was a faint ribbon of a line between sea and sky, an irrelevance for the many oystercatchers and gulls flying along the coast.

He stood up and walked to the window. The hedge barred the view of the murder scene. Perhaps that was deliberate or perhaps the house was not occupied at the time. As he returned from the window he stopped by a dark mahogany bookcase. It was not glass-enclosed. The taller books held each other up while the smaller novels sat in a regimental line on the shelf beneath. He squatted down to let his eyes wander across the vertical titles.

One caught his eye. He saw the author was Caroline Marks. The name meant nothing to him. He rarely got through three books a year. Only one of which would be a novel. He flipped through the pages, three hundred and thirty-nine of them. But the title enlarged his pupils. He read the back cover blurb in silence while his thoughts preoccupied his mind. *Hidden Bodies*, he whispered to himself in disbelief. He laid the book on top of the coffee table. He'd look at it again later. He returned to his seat and picked up the guestbook.

He dismissed the names where families had come on holiday. Children would be an inconvenience when burying a body, he concluded. He looked at couples and single visitors of which there were only a few. Then a car slowed down and stopped outside the house.

The couple waved to Rory as they passed the window. The front wooden door slammed shut. They arrived in the lounge without taking off their outside clothes.

'Got the key from the next-door neighbour, did you?' asked John.

'Yes Mrs. Hodge, Karla told me to get it from them. It's still a murder scene of course. I'll try not to let it affect your holiday.'

'You got to admit a policeman in the house isn't normal. Looks like you are after a criminal.'

'Wheesht John, he's only doing his job,' said his wife, staring daggers at her husband's out-of-place comment.

'Relax John. You need two officers to charge a criminal,' Rory said with a grin enough to relax the uptight holidaymaker.

That night Rory went to bed with two books. He laid the guest book down on his wooden bedside table and opened *Hidden Bodies*. It was almost 2 am when he turned off his bedside light.

# 6

On his desk the following morning, he saw an envelope. It wasn't opened. His secretary came in.

'Rory, that doesn't look like a run of the mill letter. It's a bit grimy. I left it for you,' she said with a shy smile. 'I hope you don't mind.'

Rory lifted his ruler and raised the letter with it. 'One for the bomb squad?' he joked.

Lorna just laughed. So did Rory. The Bomb Squad must be in Glasgow or somewhere else, he thought. Must check it out in his reference book sometime, he decided.

The rest of his mail seemed almost anticipated. Requests came flooding in to visit primary schools; the Women's Guild and Probus wished a police talk too. He would have time to answer these letters later, so he returned to the tatty letter. It contained just one sheet of paper. He unfolded it and sat back to decipher the script.

The heading was unambiguous. It referred to the murder in the field. The suggestion was that a hermit lived in the King's Cave and he would know about the body if he was not in fact the culprit. The letter was unsigned.

The King's Cave was a regular visitor's walk in the summer so any hermit living there must have been noticed by cave visitors. Yet, his whereabouts had not come to Rory's attention. But he should know if a hermit was there, what his source of nutrition, clothing, and possible income was like, why he was there and how long had he been a hermit? These were certainly matters to resolve and a trip out there was essential. He looked out of the window. The sky had a few lingering striations but no threatening clouds. It was a good day to investigate.

That afternoon, in a gentle breeze from the west, Rory left his car at the Blackwaterfoot car park and proceeded to the sandy shoreline. He could hardly believe his good fortune being the local bobby in such a picturesque part of the country. He took off his cap and let the breeze run through his wavy hair. Eventually, the golden sand gave way to rocks which slowed his progress. He glanced up and nearly stumbled on a grassy knoll hiding a bolder. His eye had caught the black silhouette of a submarine heading south on some mission. He stopped to admire its steady progress.

Within twenty minutes he was in sight of the King's Cave. He stopped and looked for any movement. There was none. He continued however in order to find out what living conditions the hermit would be experiencing in such a tricky and varied climate. He was very surprised to have heard that a hermit was actually living in the cave.

The grassy bank had long since gone and the terrain now had boulders of various sizes to negotiate. His footing was far from secure as he fought to maintain his balance as he proceeded.

A further eight minutes later he approached the first of two caves. He shouted to see if anyone was there. There was no reply. He entered the first cave and stood still. All was silent, at first. Then he heard some movement on the stony ground.

'Hi who's there?' he asked with his eyes alert and wide open.

'What do you want?' was the response.

Then from the depth of the cave, a man appeared slowly. He did not seem to be a hermit after all. He had no beard and his clothing was a warm knitted jumper and thick golden corduroy trousers. On his feet were walking boots.

'Hi, I'm Rory Murdoch the local policeman. I heard you were down here and so, I just wanted to see for myself. You know, see if you were safe if you needed anything, nothing else.'

The man stepped forward and sat down on a large boulder. Rory found a similar stone nearby and sat down beside him.

'You are not local, I'm sure of that.'

'No, well no not really,' the man said staring at the ground before him.

'So why live in a cave on Arran?'

He clasped his knees and turned towards Rory. 'I had a son. Fifteen years ago as a family we came to Carradale, across the water, on holiday,' he said as he pointed to the land across the Kilbranan Sound.

Rory nodded his head encouraging him to say more.

'It was the first time we had been to Carradale.'

Rory saw tears welling up in the man's eyes. His voice spoke with a quiver.

'It was a sunny afternoon and Paul my son, was loaned a boat, well not really a boat, a blown-up plastic thing with two paddles. I kept an eye on him as he went round in circles in the safety of the protecting arm of the walled harbour.'

'I know exactly where you are, I've been to Carradale a few times myself.'

He looked at me. 'Have you any children?'

'Yes, I have got a daughter.'

'Grown-up and making her way in life? A solicitor or a psychologist perhaps?'

'No, actually she's at home, in a wheelchair. She has spina bifida. She's in her teens.'

'I am sorry to hear that,' he said sincerely as he reflected on his inappropriate suggestions.

'Carradale, you were saying....'

'Yes. The wind got up and I gathered the picnic things. I was almost set to get off the beach when I turned round and saw neither Paul nor the boat. I could not understand why. Then I assumed he had sailed round the harbour and was on the other side of the wall. That could be the only solution. I ran towards the harbour and mounted the steps. I looked out over the sound and saw nothing. I called out his name and was met by silence.'

Rory unbuttoned his high-visibility jacket. 'Did you call the police?'

'Police, ambulance, fire brigade, mountain rescue, and boy scouts all searched the coastline for days. I couldn't have expected a better turnout. But nothing, absolutely nothing.'

'Devastating. So, you come here to search......?'

'After the holiday I returned to Glasgow, a broken man. Lost an eleven-year-old son. But I did not lose hope that one day, I'd return to be with him.'

'So you have not been here long?'

'Six weeks, just a day or two over.'

Rory stood up. He gazed out to the calm water between the island and Carradale. Then he turned towards the man. 'I'm Rory.'

The man shook his hand. 'I'm Ron, Ron Glover.'

There was a lingering smile between the two men as they separated.

'So why did you come here, Rory?' he asked.

'Oh, it does not matter.'

'To me it does.'

Rory looked away from him and took a deep breath. 'There's been a body found, a female, and I wondered if you knew anything about it. But if you have only been here a short time, you could not know about her. The body has been in the ground for over a year.' He smiled at him conscious that his visit was now so unnecessary. 'So, what work did you have before you retired?'

'Thought you might have guessed.'

'Er no,' Rory said with his eyebrows joined.

'I was a Police sergeant.'

'A sergeant in the police?' he said raising his voice in surprise.

The man nodded. 'You heard me right.'

Rory picked up two stones and threw them at a rock in the cave.

'You're no hermit then. You'll have a police pension.'

'Who said I was a hermit?' asked Ron.

Rory remembered the letter was not signed. 'Just heard there was someone in the cave and came to the wrong conclusion.'

'So, this is like a social visit then?'

Rory nodded his agreement. 'You know, I'm really at a loss with this skeleton found just outside Blackwaterfoot. Thought if you had been here for some time, you might have seen something. But obviously wrong timescale.'

'Looking like a cold case.'

'Aye Ron, a very cold case.

# 7

Rory was satisfied that his police pension provided Ron with the food he needed and he learned he had a home on the island near Pirnmill. Maybe it was perhaps more of a mental health issue. One to mention to the clinic nurse, next time she called to see Ella.

When he returned from the cave, his secretary met him with what she described as a development.

'Rory,' said Lorna, 'there's an important envelope on your desk. Mind you open it. It was delivered by a cycle courier.'

Rory threw his hat onto the peg at the back of his door and smiled. He often missed. He saw the brown envelope which had excited Lorna. He sat at his desk and lifted a bamboo letter opener, slicing through the end in seconds.

He pulled out all the pages and staring at him was a young woman. He read on.

The letter was from D.I. Sammy Grant:

'A bid to identify the woman's body found in a field at Kilpatrick near Blackwaterfoot has taken a turn for the better. The work from Liverpool John Moore's University has provided us with a facial reconstruction of a woman based on the remains of her body. The woman is estimated to be young to middle-aged, about 4 ft 11 inches tall, that should be small, and around 8.5 stones.'

Rory was ordered to have this picture copied and posted in every town and village on the island. He looked at the picture closely. Naturally, he felt sorry for the girl. He vowed she would get justice one day.

He prepared a covering letter and sent it with a picture of the girl to the police offices around the island with extra photos for shop windows. Rory hoped it might prompt someone with some memory of her, no matter how distant or unlikely.

He sat back content that the case had moved on a fraction and drank his afternoon tea. He looked out of the window and found the blue sky freckled with striated clouds. The sun shone through the window and heated his desk. He looked at the office clock. Just an hour and a half before he ended his day.

Then he received a telephone call. It was from the cook at the Blackwaterfoot Hotel. Another body, this timed a clothed body had been washed up on the beach nearby. It was apparently a young girl and recently deceased. Yet another murder! Arran would not be a tourist attraction if there were any more bodies, he thought. Yet, he felt he had much more to go on in this case.

The girl's body was half in the water, half out. Rory called for assistance from the Lochranza police station and Constable Colin Nelson joined him a good half hour later. They brought the corpse onto the beach. Colin looked at her sullen face. He suddenly stopped in his tracks.

'What's up Colin?'

'I prefer to be called Nelson. You know, Nelson, the sea Lord,' he said as his puzzled look fixed on the soaked body.

'Well okay but as I said, what's up?' Rory asked keeping his mind on the victim and his eye on his colleague.

Nelson turned towards Rory shaking his head in disbelief. 'I know this girl.'

'You sure?' asked Rory.

'Damn sure I am. This is Lizzie Dynes, from Corrie. My daughter and Lizzie were in primary school together. But Lizzie didn't go to the High School at Lamlash. She stayed with her Gran in Largs, on the mainland. Aye, I'm pretty sure of that.'

'So her parents are still in Corrie?'

'No, they separated. Mother moved to Lochranza a few years ago. I know the house.'

The ambulance arrived and took the body to the mortuary in Brodick. The pathologist's initial report showed death not by drowning but death by strangulation. Rory had another murder case to solve.

Armed with a photo of the deceased on his mobile, Rory and Constable Nelson made their way to Lochranza and the home of the victim. On ringing the front doorbell, a woman appeared with her mouth agape at seeing two police officers on her front doorstep.

'May we come in? We have some bad news for you, I'm afraid,' said Rory taking off his cap.

They were taken into a neat and tidy front room with a picture of her daughter on the mantelpiece. Rory had already made the connection. He opened his phone and found the victim's picture. 'Can you identify who this is?' he asked with gravitas as he handed the mobile phone over to her.

Naturally, she responded with tears and sobs. Rory did not press her. After some thirty seconds, she spoke.

'Where....where did you find her? Which part of London?'

'London?' asked Constable Nelson in surprise. 'She was found on the shore at Blackwaterfoot.'

Mrs. Dynes looked at the photo once more straining to see the picture clearly through dribbling tears.

'But she was in London. She went to London last week.'

'What did she do in London?' asked a confused Rory.

'She went to her cousin at Muswell Hill. She was going to stay with her in north London till she got a job. She was keen to get a city life experience.'

The officers looked at one another. Rory broke the silence. 'Where is Mr. Dynes?'

'There's no Mr. Dynes. We parted two years ago.'

'So, there's no man in the house?'

'Well, we're no married. Jim lives with me.'

'That's Jim who?' asked Constable Nelson.

'Jim Randall.' Rory felt he was making progress but wondered how loyal Mrs. Dynes might be to her new relationship.

'Then Jim Randall is the step-father of Lizzie?' he asked to ensure clarity.

Mrs. Dynes nodded and wrung her hands.

'So how did Lizzie get on with Jim?' asked Rory.

Mrs. Dynes looked up at the ceiling as if in prayer.

'They had their moments. But London? I just can't believe this. There's something not right here.'

'Had their moments, what exactly do you mean?' questioned Rory.

'I suppose like any teenage daughter with a step-Dad. There was some tension.'

'Tension?'

'Yes, arguments that sort of thing,'

'Did Jim lay his hands on her at any time?'

'From time to time,' she replied to Rory without hesitation.

'Did you ever call the police about him?'

'Oh no, I couldn't do that.'

'Wouldn't or couldn't,' Constable Nelson tried to clarify.

The questions were raining down on her and had to be thought through. Anxiety was etched on her face. She chose not to answer for a moment.

'Jim ran her to the ferry when she was leaving for London. That shows he was caring.'

'When was that?'

'Let me see. That would be last Thursday, yes, last week, four days ago,' she said drying her eyes with her soggy handkerchief.

'And Jim took her to the ferry?'

She nodded her agreement amid sobs.

Rory's eyes met Nelson's. The passenger list would be easily obtained, was what they seemed to be thinking.

'Was there a party the day before Lizzie left home?'

'Why do you ask?' she demanded sharply.

'Well, it is a big thing leaving home, leaving friends, the sort of occasion I thought a party might be on the cards.'

Mrs. Dynes nodded. 'Lizzie wanted a farewell party but Jim was having none of it,' she informed them in a long, drawn-out sentence.

'Why was that?' asked Rory.

'Och, I don't really know. He has such a temper.'

'So where is Jim now?'

'He'll be home soon, it will be dark. He's a clam fisherman.'

'Does he have his own boat?' asked Rory.

'Oh yes, he's self-employed.'

Mrs. Dynes made tea and they all sat at the table to drink it as their police car remained stationed outside. The sobs eventually subsided but through glazed eyes, Mrs. Dynes still could not understand why her daughter was not in London.

Rory looked outside the window at the car and shook his head. 'Looks like he's late or he's seen the car perhaps and is keeping away. Would that be likely?'

'Well I suppose so,' she said. 'I mean wouldn't you if a police car were outside your door?'

Rory silently agreed with her and left to move his car behind her house out of sight. On his way back to her house, he stopped. He pulled from his pocket his mobile.

Rory phoned his superior D.I. Sammy Grant on the mainland that evening and advised him of what he knew about this second murder to cross his path.

'So, what's your plan of action now?'

'We'll hang on till Jim comes home from his fishing and bring him in for questioning.'

There was a two-second pause. 'Nonsense. Get home have a good night's sleep and then go out to arrest him in the morning'

'Er....'

'No errs about it, get a good night's sleep.'

Rory's mobile changed ears. 'But what happens if he gets home and she tells him the police have been calling? Should we not wait awhile and even arrest him tonight, if need be?'

'God, man! Do you not hear me? It's bloody Arran. He's not going far, is he?'

Rory looked in disbelief at his phone. 'Good night sir,' he managed to say but there was no reply.

# 8

The following morning was dry but the sky was almost cloudy grey. The wind was getting up and Rory saw flecks of breaking waves in the bay. It looked like worse weather would soon arrive. He hoped the day would go by quickly.

He rang Nelson at the Lochranza police station. 'I'll be over in forty minutes. I'll have a coffee with you before we pick him up, Okay?'

Sounds good to me.'

An uneventful trip to Lochranza was made under an increasing drizzle. However, as he entered the town he smiled. The deer were in the fairway of the local golf course as usual. They were resident there. How golfers negotiated these moveable obstacles left Rory wondering. Golf was not his sport. His sporting days were over. *Match of the Day* was the sport his domestic life would permit.

He drove into the police car park and as he got out of his car, he sniffed the air. Coffee was waiting.

'So, what do we know about this step-father, Jim Randall?'

'He's not a local for a start. Ex-marine, fit sort of guy. He's had a few scrapes, assaults in fights. He's done a stretch of six months at Her Majesty's pleasure,' said Nelson pouring two coffees.

'In jail for what?'

Nelson put his mug down. He consulted a file. 'He had in his possession an eight-inch kitchen knife in a public place. It would have been fatal, if he used it. He got done for possession of a weapon with intent to harm. He was lucky it was not murder. That was in central Glasgow, of course.'

'Good. Seems we'll have our hands full. Got any tasers here?' asked Rory.

'Tasers? Do you think we've ever needed a taser on Arran before?'

'Then I hope he co-operates with us,' said Rory adjusting his hat.

They swallowed their last dregs of coffee and Rory visited the loo.

On his return, he looked at his watch. 9:06 am. As they drove the short way to the house, Rory smiled. 'I bet he's in bed still.'

Nelson smiled back but said nothing.

They parked outside the house and made their way up the drive. Rory gave a firm knock on the door as he prepared for the response. His knock was met with silence. He knocked again more firmly and with more wraps on the door. He looked round at Nelson and pointed to the window. Nelson went to the window and peered in.

'It's a bit of a mess in the lounge.'

'What do you mean,' asked a worried-looking Rory, remembering what it looked like the day before.

'Looks like some sort of disturbance.'

'Let me see.'

Rory being an inch or two taller than Nelson shaded his eyes against the glass window from a higher vantage point. 'It's not how we left it last night. I don't like this. I think we had better gain access and see what else we find.' Nelson nodded.

They returned to the front door and peered through the letterbox. They had a greater excuse to enter now. The bottom step seemed to have drying blood on it.

They combed through each ground floor room. The kitchen gave nothing away. As they did so, they called out Jim Randall's name. There was no response. The dining room was in order. They mounted the stairs with their hands on their truncheons.

At the top of the stairs, they entered a bedroom. It was a box room with nowhere to hide. Then Nelson gave Rory a poke on the ribs and pointed to the far away bedroom. Blood was on the door handle.

They walked cautiously along the carpeted corridor and Rory opened the door. 'Come out with your hands on your head,' he commanded. They stood still listening for any movement. Rory then placed his left foot against the door and began to enter.

Immediately he saw a naked foot on the ground. He entered further and saw the dead body of Mrs. Dynes. Her head was red with dried blood. He approached her and confirmed the body was deceased.

Rory turned toward Nelson with his lips tightly gathered. He shook his head. 'You know why we did not arrest him last night?'

'The car was in sight?'

'No, because I was instructed to get a good night's sleep. There would have been no murder if we had waited for him. I blame that stupid inspector Grant for this unnecessary murder.'

They returned to Lochranza police station each with their own thoughts. Rory got on the phone to D.I. Sammy Grant.

'Sir, we have another murder on our hands.'

'What the hell is going on there, on Arran?'

'We are the masters of our own downfall. You told me to return home and arrest him this morning,' said Rory with his blood boiling and his neck turning red,

'Well, didn't you?'

'Your order was incompetent,' he continued. 'We have the murderer on the run. His partner and her daughter have been killed. This is the reality. We need a couple of police dogs here and more police if we are to catch this man. He may murder again. He's got a violent record.'

There was a pause. Grant chose not to reply to the incompetence insult or Rory's outburst. 'I'm coming over and we'll get you a dog and police staff.' The call was ended abruptly.

Rory looked at Nelson. 'Okay, let's look for some of his clothing and bag it. The dog will need a scent to go on.'

'Socks, I'd go for eh?' asked Nelson.'

# 9

Rory was at the ferry terminal to see the ship edge its way towards the quay the following morning. The air was fresh and the clouds minimal. The sea glistened in its blue cape while seagulls dived between stout rocks on the shore. Dog walkers were ubiquitous with a variety of small, medium-sized dogs and a Bernese mountain dog on a stout black lead walked stately beside its scruffy owner. The dog's slavers dribbled down from its open mouth, as this breed tends to do.

Grant's first words were hardly welcoming. 'Got the house secured?'

'Of course,' said Rory on edge.

'Then take me to it,' he said lifting his mobile to his ear instructing some other to do his will.

When they got to Lochranza, there was a strong smell of sea-weed in the air. Rory looked towards the outskirts of the town and saw two police caravans arriving.

'I see we've got the cavalry,' he said within Grant's earshot.

'No holiday for them. They are the first to arrive. There will be three detectives, two senior investigating officers, manhunt specialists, blood splatter analysts, dog handlers, interviewing officers, crime-scene managers, a phone analyst and one of the force's lawyers is on his way.'

Rory gave a sly look at Nelson whose face seemed about to break out in a laugh.

'Seriously depleting your Ayrshire staff sir,' said Rory.

Inspector Grant frowned at Rory. 'Never heard of Police Scotland? Your employer? There's no Ayrshire police. This is a top squad you are lucky to have and don't forget it.'

Rory gulped. 'Then what's our role, me and Nelson?'

'Bloody obvious to me. Find accommodation pronto. Get me a room with a sea view. Don't bother about the two plainclothes officers at the terminals.''

'Terminals?'

'Yes, of course, Brodick and Claonaig. Good God, do you live in space?'

'But sir it's 20$^{th}$ October,' said Rory.

'Oh my. It's yer birthday I take it,' Grant said with a smirk of derision.

'No sir. There's no winter sailing to Claonaig after 18$^{th}$ October.'

Grant seemed to ignore the advice given by Rory looking toward the desolate landing area of the Lochranza ferry. Then came a moment of clarity, in his own mind. 'He could have taken his boat. He's a clam fisherman isn't he?'

'He might have. But look. Third craft from the left, on the grassy bank. That red boat there; it's his clam-fishing boat.'

A further moment of silence as Grant found Rory's answers true, but irritating.

'Just one thing, sir. Who is in charge of all this team?'

'Less of your cheek. It's obvious, isn't it? I am. Now find accommodation at the B&B going rate. Then get a supply of lunches for us at 1 pm. Got it?'

Rory nodded with a sigh of despair. Grant turned to gaze at him. Rory caught his stare and responded appropriately. 'Yes, sir. We've got it,' he said turning towards Nelson and ushering him on their way.

Both officers made for the Lochranza Hotel. Situated in a dominant position overlooking the bay and set just off the main road, the building sat in its proud position.

No sooner was Nelson in the lounge when the friendly manageress appeared.

'Hi, bit early for lunch but can I rustle up something for you, Colin.'

'No, we're here on business Angela,' said Nelson with a wink.

She hesitated. She put her head to one side. It was a coquette gesture. 'Business with me? She sat down.

'What do you mean business?'

'Business, just that,' said Rory. 'Can you provide fourteen lunches? Probably for the next few days?'

'And your friend, Colin. Does he have a name?'

'Sorry, this is Rory based in Lamlash, usually.'

'I see. I like what he's asking. You've never asked for such an order Colin,' she laughed. Then a realisation hit her hard.

'It's about the murder, of course, isn't it?'

'Yes. A double murder. Don't forget their daughter.' Nelson stroked his chin. 'Angela, you wouldn't know where Mr. Jim Randall might be?'

She scratched her head. 'You know, come to think about it, I saw Jim on the night of the murder,' she said untying her apron.

The officers sat down at a table and Rory took out his notebook. 'You were saying, you saw him?'

Angela sat opposite them and sighed so huge her hands hardly covered her mouth. 'Yes....it was about 9.30 pm. He got on his bike and I thought, where was he going at that time?'

'Which direction was that?'

'South, down past the Youth Hostel.'

Rory licked the tip of his pencil. 'And what colour of bike?'

'A man's bike, of course, you know with the horizontal bar. It was blue and silver, with a mud flap behind the front wheel. Can I get you lads coffee?

Nelson smiled and answered in the affirmative. Rory kept on writing but nodded as he did so.

'Alice, three coffees please,' Angela shouted out behind her hand, to the cook. In the distance, they heard her repeat the order.

Rory looked up. 'You know that makes you a witness.'

Angela laughed. 'That makes it so official.'

Rory scratched his ear. I suppose I'd better get that off to the boss. But first how many rooms do you have available?'

Angela shook her head. None, for the next three days. I've a party of ornithologists from Wales here and two elderly women up for a week, from Surbiton. Sorry.'

Rory tapped in the number and he waited. D.I. Grant grunted. 'Yes?'

'Sir, Jim Randall left his house last night at about 9.30 pm and cycled down the east coast on a blue and silver bicycle.'

'Who told you?' he asked abruptly.

'The manageress of the hotel, where we are.'

'What are you doing at the hotel? Having lunch I presume and not getting on with the bookings.'

'No sir, interviewing the manageress and booking rooms.'

'Don't forget to get me a room with a good view of the sea, at the hotel.'

'Sorry, sir, all fully booked. We'll find you somewhere else.'

'Get on with it,' he said in a growl and switched off his phone.

D.I. Grant lost no time in instructing two officers to get into an unmarked car and set off south to find the cyclist. Meanwhile, he telephoned the ferry terminal at Brodick where he had two officers in plain clothes telling them to look out for Jim Randall's escape from the island.

Meanwhile, Rory was thinking hard. A devious smile came over him.

'Tell me Angela, you know the bed and breakfast outlets around here?'

'Yes, I know them all. We are in touch when we get an influx of visitors just like today.'

Rory glanced at Nelson then winked at him.

'If a difficult and nasty customer came to you here for a night, and you had no vacancies, where would you send him?'

Angela laughed at the thought. 'Send him? No problem. Mrs. McMaster would be the place for him.'

'And why is that?'

'Mrs. McMaster is a nosy besom. She's well into her seventies and has what I might say; some... er body hygiene issues?'

'You mean she is fat?' asked Rory.

'Fat? No, she's not fat. A bit overweight perhaps but not fat. Let me just say soap and water does not come into contact with her as often as it should. Body odours, I'd say but please don't quote me on that. Mind you a superb view down the sea loch, she has. One of the best.'

Nelson smiled from ear to ear.

Rory sat back with the smile of a Cheshire cat.

'Excellent, just what he ordered. Can I ask you to contact her and see if she might take D.I. Samuel Grant?'

'Isn't a D.I. quite important?'

'Yes, in his own eyes. But I think we all have a gripe about him. Anyway, he asked for a good sea view, and that's what he's gonna get, eh Nelson?' Rory said with contentment etched over his smiling face.

Angela stood up and went to a chest of drawers. She returned with a list of all hostelries and B&B venues around Lochranza.

'Why don't I contact all of them?' asked Rory.

'Better I do it. They know me.'

'I suppose that makes sense,' said Rory, slapping both knees with the palm of his hands for making such a ridiculous suggestion.

'How many rooms do you need? Any married?'

'I don't know of any married couples in this lot of experts but there will be a need for eleven beds. Fourteen of us in all, in fact, but Nelson is a local of course, I'll need to return to Lamlash and D.I. Grant has already got his heavenly abode with Mrs. McMaster, not so?'

'Indeed he has,' said Angela feeling excited to be part of the plot.

'So can you make a list of the remainder and phone me when they are all ready. I'll need them by 5 pm?'

'No problem. Glad to help out.'

'Thanks, Angela,' said Nelson and Rory stood and shook her hand. 'You have been a great help, more than a help in fact.'

'Oh and fourteen lunches?' reminded Rory.

'No sooner said than done. I'll set them out in the bar. It's the largest area.'

'Great. Accommodation and meals. Just what the D.I. ordered,' said Nelson feeling satisfied to be complicit in the deception with a job well done.

# 10

Rory returned his reading glasses to a uniform pocket and fixed his sunglasses securely over his nose. They entered the hotel car park and simultaneously took in a lungful of fresh sea air.

'Trouble being Police Scotland, I suppose they could transfer us anywhere,' said Nelson.

'They'd be hard-hearted if they did that to me. I'm Ella's primary carer.'

Nelson nodded thoughtfully. 'Of course,' he said.

'Fancy a wee run in the car?' asked Rory glad not to be concentrating on his paternal duties till he got home.

'Anywhere specific?'

'Perhaps we can mosey on down the coast at a gentle pace. I guess they will have sent some fast car down to catch Jim Randall. Let's take our time for half an hour then return for lunch and let everyone know where they are staying.'

'Sounds good to me but I hope your plan does not backfire'

'How could it. The instruction was a sea view and a bedroom. We delivered. We could hardly inspect all the accommodation,' said a smug and satisfied Rory.

Within seven minutes they were on the coast road heading towards the village of Sannox. They let cars overtake them as they casually made their way south. Soon they came to Corrie where they parked in the car park of the Corrie Hotel. They stretched their legs and arms and set off to the rocky beach to recharge their human batteries. They had no intention of engaging in idle Corrie chatter with the locals at the hotel that day. They made their way onto the rocks; some seemed slippery and they avoided them. Their focus was no more than a foot ahead of their police issued boots. They found a flat dry rock and sat down. Ahead of them was the Clyde and in the distance, a tanker seemed to move south as slowly as a tortoise. Was it going to America or further south to Argentina? Rory aired his thoughts.

'Probably going to Belfast,' was Nelson's response, and Rory, on reflection, felt it more likely as well. They took their high-visibility jackets off and laid back to enjoy the sun's warm rays.

Nelson stretched out to make him comfortable but Rory was ill at ease. He sat up and clung to his knees in a seated position.

'That D.I. gets me down.' He said, 'He seems to have it in for me. The sooner this murder gets solved and he's back on dry land the better. He's just not Arran material. I guess he'll rub a few more feathers the wrong way before he leaves.'

'Just my thoughts too, Rory.'

Then Rory peered over his glasses for a moment's reflection then focussed his gaze. He nudged his colleague.

'Over there,' he pointed with an outstretched finger.

'Over where?' Nelson replied rubbing his eyes.

'There.' Rory raised his voice in excitement and his pointed finger shook.

'You mean beyond that rock by the water's edge?'

'Yes a wheel, a tyre. Let's suss it out.'

They cautiously stepped over rocks in the direction they had identified. They walked nearer the sea over wetter stones. It took the best part of four minutes before they saw the silver handlebars and the blue frame.

'Any sight of Randall?' asked Nelson.

They scanned the coastline making sure their eyes did not miss anything untoward. Then they focussed on the sea for a body.

'The tide is low just now. If he had drowned, his body would be south of here,' stated Nelson.

'Yes, it would but.... what if this bike...is a decoy?

'Hmmm' said Nelson. 'Interesting thought you have there. But for me? That's one for the big boys back in Lochranza.'

Rory took his mobile phone from his tunic pocket. He dialled the D.I.

'Sir, we've found Randall's bike.'

A moment's silence ensued.

'Sir, I said we've found Randall's bike.'

'I heard you the first time. Where is it?'

'On the rocky shore at Corrie.'

'Corrie? What the hell are you doing there?'

'Local knowledge sir, following our instinct?'

'I thought I told you to find accommodation not to go gallivanting around the island.'

`Sir with respect, the list of addresses is being prepared as we speak. We have already secured a sea view for you, sir. You will have it just around 5 pm and lunch at just after 1 pm. Meantime we followed our local instinct as I told you and found Randall's bike. I thought that might please you,' said Rory as Nelson noticed his face turn red once more with rage.

'Pleasing me is beside the point. I'll send two scenes of crime officers over. Stay where you are and show them the bike.'

'Yes sir,' said Rory although the D.I. had already turned off his phone. 'I wonder if Mrs. McMaster has a sister.'

Nelson's face contorted. 'Why?'

'Well he won't want a second night with Mrs. McMaster and I'd love to see him lodged with a McMaster relative if he wants a move.'

Their laughs merged with the screeching of the diving cormorants.

They sat down again on a warm flat stone.

'This is the life, Rory.'

'Yeah - let nobody take it away from us.'

# 11

The Scenes of Crime officers arrived, relieving both Nelson and Murdoch after they had informed the latter how they had come across the bike and had confirmed there was no sight of Mr. Randall.

They made their way back to the hotel in Lochranza where Angela greeted them. They sat down at a table in the bar for a late lunch and a folder was brought to their attention. Rory opened it and saw the list of landladies with the numbers of rooms they offered. There was also a map of Lochranza with each B&B highlighted.

'And Mrs. McMaster was happy to have the D.I.?' asked Rory.

'Happy? She was flustered. She had not had a lodger in the last nine months.'

'Well thank you, Angela, I guess we'd better get on our way to reassure the team that they all have ideal accommodation,' said Rory folding the list and placing it in his pocket as he pushed his empty sandwich plate further onto the table with his other hand.

The police had set up their headquarters in the foreground of Lochranza Castle. A large white tent was their focus and the officers made their way to their colleagues.

Rory entered and found a pinboard. He placed the map of the town on it and sat down to allocate the team's accommodation. First was to ensure D.I. Grant got his comeuppance. Then the others were easily divided. The female staff had adjoining accommodation and the male numbers fitted into the remaining homes. All accepted their lot. Just as he was finishing, D.I. Grant approached.

'Got everyone bedded?' he asked.

'Yes sir. Let me show where you are.' Rory took his superior officer to the town map. He raised his finger to identify his dwelling for the duration of the enquiry. He could see a smile start to change on his solemn face.

'Good position. Just at the head of the loch. Sun should be in the right place in the morning. Looks like you have done well Murdoch, or was it Nelson who found it with his local knowledge?'

'Angela at the hotel did the donkey work. All we did was find the missing bike.' Rory placed his hands on his hips. 'May I ask a question, sir?'

D.I. Grant turned towards Rory Murdoch.

Rory first took a deep breath and he was aware his heart was pounding at pace. 'Why did I not get the staff when I needed it for the body in the field at Kirkpatrick?' The atmosphere changed. There was a sharpness in the air and the full force of anger came Rory's way.

'You made no bloody progress with that murder did you? I mean, not enough grafting for evidence, or seeking more input. That case is dead and buried. You'll never get to the bottom of that one. I did not want you to foul up the child murder. That's why I'm the D.I. and you are not, Murdoch. We'll get Randall mark my words. It's a matter of time.'

As Grant walked away, Rory looked at his watch. He decided to head for Lamlash and some sanity.

'Till tomorrow then. We'll see how the sparks fly then.'

'Yup, it's been an interesting day. I'm for home soon but not the pub tonight. I guess it will be full of our lot, and that might include Grant,' Nelson said giving Rory a friendly thump on the back.

# 12

Rory entered his home with heavy steps. He was dead beat. Flop ran to greet him and he rubbed the spaniel's ears.

'Ella, sorry I'm late. I've been to Lochranza today.'

There was no reply. He threw his jacket over the staircase post and went into the lounge. The TV was on. He noticed Ella slumped in her chair. He approached her and tapped her shoulder. She turned towards him with a faint smile.

Her smile lit the room. 'Hi, Dad, can you straighten me up?'

Rory stood behind his daughter and raised her on her chair, pulling her back. This effort made him breathe laboriously.

'There's a letter for you, over there. It's from the nurse today.'

Rory saw the letter on the settee. He sat down and opened it.

**Dear Mr. Murdoch**

**Re Ella**

**I have to tell you Dr. Black and I have been assessing Ella's movement. We feel it is in her best interest that she should have some beneficial surgery. Let me explain in greater detail.**

In addition to the abnormal sensation and paralysis, Ella has another neurological complication associated with her Spina Bifida, which is Chiari II Malformation - a condition common in children and adolescents with Myelomeningocele - in which the brain stem and the cerebellum (hindbrain) protrude downward into the spinal canal or neck area.

This condition can lead to compression of the spinal cord and cause a variety of symptoms including difficulties with feeding, swallowing, and breathing control; choking; and changes in upper arm function (stiffness, weakness). We need not remind you that Ella has many of these symptoms.

Chiari II malformation seems to have resulted in a blockage of cerebrospinal fluid in Ella. It is causing a condition called Hydrocephalus, which is an abnormal build-up of cerebrospinal fluid in and around the brain. This is what we feel Ella suffering from most. Cerebrospinal fluid is a clear liquid that surrounds the brain and spinal cord. The build-up of fluid puts damaging pressure on these structures. Hydrocephalus is commonly treated by surgically implanting a shunt—a hollow tube—in the brain to drain the excess fluid into the abdomen.

I am sorry my explanation seems very medical but in essence, before Ella grows any older, a

**shunt would be in her best interest to improve the quality of her life.**

**As her parent, of course, you could deny surgery. However, I would urge you to consider Dr. Black's conclusion.**

**Do not hesitate to call either Dr. Black or myself if you wish to discuss this letter further.**

**Yours**
**Maggie Ritchie**
**Senior nursing sister**
**SB Specialist**

Rory placed the letter back in its envelope and sat down beside his daughter. He brushed her hair back and stroked her forehead.

'Do you know what they have written?' he asked.

'Yes, they want to give me an operation.'

Rory nodded. 'And what do you think about that idea, darling?'

'I don't know. Will it hurt? Will you come to the hospital with me?'

'Of course, I'll be with uou and it won't hurt. They will give you a general anaesthetic. You won't feel a thing. Are you are sure you want to go ahead with the operation?'

Ella's eyes looked soulful. She put out her hand to hold her father's. 'I know it won't make me better but it will make me more comfortable. Won't it?'

A tear trickled down Rory's cheek. He cuddled his daughter. 'I only want the very best for you, pet.'

'I know Dad. I know you do.'

Rory stood up and closed the curtains. 'I got some fresh fish from Brodick.'

Ella smiled. Rory set off to the kitchen.

The following morning, sitting at his office desk, he telephoned Maggie Ritchie.

'Hi, Maggie. I got your letter. Er...so you think an op is best for Ella, eh?'

'Yes, it is the right time for it. A shunt should make her quality of life a good bit better.'

'Should?' Rory shot off.

'Well, it is a general anaesthetic. There's always a slight risk but if she was my daughter, I'd go for it.'

That was what Rory needed to hear.

'So when would the op be?'

'Two weeks on Monday. You'd have to take her up to Glasgow on Sunday night.'

Rory flipped through his diary. 'Monday 18th?'

'Yes, so be up mid-afternoon on the day before. There are quite a few B&B's nearby.'

Rory's face contorted. 'You mean I can't stay with Ella in the hospital?'

'Once she's out of the theatre, you can stay with her in the recovery ward. There's a settee that folds down. You can spend the night there if you need to. But it's her age, she may be seen as too old to have a parent share her ward. You'll have to ask.'

'Okay, I've got the date in my diary. Thanks.'

He replaced the handset and went to boil the kettle. He prepared his mug of coffee. As the kettle boiled he realised the D.I. would have to grant him leave. With his mug at the table, he lifted the phone and dialled D.I. Grant.

'Rory Murdoch here. I'd like to take the week beginning 18th off.' He got the request off his chest.

'For the first time in your career you have three murders on your plate and you want to bloody well go on holiday. Christ, you are the pits.'

'But sir, you don't....'

'Don't understand? You think I arrived in a banana boat? Yes, I understand very well. You are a shirker, that's what you are Murdoch, a shirker.'

'But sir, it's not a holiday...' but his words went unheeded. D.I. Grant had spoken and as far as he was concerned, that was that.

Rory buried his head in his hands and sobbed. His cries were heard by his secretary who entered his room. Lorna approached him and placed her hands on his shoulders.

'Can you tell me what's hurting?'

Rory's eyes were red and wet. He took a sigh then recalled his last twenty-four hours, leaving out nothing so Lorna was fully appraised.

'If I could only get two minutes with your D.I., I'd give him an earful,' she said thumping the table with her fist.

'I'd better get up to Lochranza. I'll have to see him myself,' he said wiping his tears with his handkerchief.

'You'll do no such thing. You are under too much stress. Go see Dr. Black he knows what's going on and he's bound to give you sick leave. Don't worry about here. We'll manage. Now finish your coffee and I'll make an appointment for you to see Dr. Black.'

Rory felt the impact of Lorna's suggestion. He had never had a day's illness in his life. Yet, why was he buckling under the D.I.?

Lorna returned to his room smiling. 'If you go now, Dr. Black can see you.'

Within forty-five minutes Rory had returned to his office and announced that he had been given three weeks off, due to stress.

Lorna reassured him that she'd get through all the paperwork and would help his colleagues as much as she could. It was unlikely that anyone would be brought in to fill the void.

'I'll e-mail the D.I. I'll lay it on thick and true. Now off you go, and give my love to Ella.'

With a gentle smile, Rory patted Lorna on her arm. He had cause to be pleased. Ella's appointment at the hospital was now part of his sick leave.

# 13

Clunk click. On the Saturday before the operation, some mail hit the hall rug with a dud thud.

'Postman has been, Dad.'

'I'll be down in a moment, darling,' shouted her father as his razor cleared the last patch of shaving foam from his chin.

Rory wiped the razor on a facecloth, washed his face then dried it on the handrail towel. As he descended the staircase, he noticed the pile of mail by the door, much larger than usual. He bent down and picked them up. He entered the dining room and placed the letters on the table.

'Two are for you, darling.'

'Oh, read them to me please.'

'Both are cards.'

Indeed, one was from Rory's sister, Joan, in Kirriemuir and another from a neighbour, both wishing Ella a successful operation in Glasgow. Their neighbour two doors down looked forward to her coming home to Lamlash.

'That's kind of them, isn't it?'

'Yes Dad,' replied Ella shaking her hands in the air in excitement.

Rory put aside a football pools envelope and picked up a brown envelope. It had a Police Scotland label on the back. He opened the letter with a kitchen knife and the white paper emerged unscathed. He read it in silence. He read it again. D.I. Sammy Grant was the author of the letter and he had suspended Rory. He was not to return to work on account of his insolence and lack of professional conduct. A hearing would be initiated as soon as practicable. If he chose to retire, he would receive a police pension and not require a hearing. That did not soften the blow. Rory had not yet completed his thirty years of service by some three months. He was also instructed to hand in his uniform and any other police equipment he might have, to the Lamlash station.

Ella was aware of the silence. 'What's up? Bad news?' she asked.

Rory turned to face her. 'I've been suspended. I guess that means sacked.'

'Suspended, what does that mean?'

'It means I am no longer a policeman.'

At first, Ella smiled. It meant her father would be at home now but she saw her father's face and it told her another story. He was clearly not pleased with this news.


That afternoon Rory made his way to Lamlash police station with a Tesco bag filled with his police-issued clothes. In another firmer bag were his boots. He entered the station and was met by Lorna. She saw him place his bags on the counter. His boots made a clatter.

'What's all this, Rory?'

'I've retired from the police.'

'Oh dear! You will be sorely missed. Have you made the right decision?' she asked tilting her head to one side with a smile.

'I should be more honest with you. It was not my decision. I've been suspended by D.I. Grant.'

'My God, whatever for?'

'His words were: 'insolence and lack of professionalism.'

'You being insolent and you unprofessional? I just can't believe this. I smell a rat.'

Rory smiled and nodded. 'Give me a line to Nelson at Lochranza, please.'

Rory took the call at his old desk. He explained the letter he had received from D.I. Grant and announced he was no longer participating in any murder enquiries.

'Hey Rory, that can't be true,' he said in a tone much higher and louder than he had heard his colleague speak before.

'Yes, true it is.'

'Unprofessional? He can't have grounds for that. Insolent? He's got the wrong guy. Rory, you've got to prepare yourself for a case of unfair dismissal. I'll back you all the way. That bugger Grant should get dismissed, not you.'

Rory's smile was not detected. 'Maybe, Nelson. But I've got other things on my mind. Let me deal with these first.'

'Sure, my prayers are for you and Ella but Rory, this is a case of unfair dismissal, mark my words,' he said banging his boot on the floor. 'I'll get the word around up here. Grant will get frosted out if I have my way.'

'Thanks. Oh by the way, how is Grant enjoying his B&B?'

'He's forgone the fine view. He's in a room at the back of the hotel. Angela saw to that, the very back. His bedroom view is facing a stone wall.'

That gave some comfort to Rory. 'Well, come visit when you are down this way.'

'I sure will. Let me take your dismissal up with the police federation. I'll let you know what they say.'

'Er...okay....yup.... thanks, Nelson.'

There was a knock on his door. Lorna placed her head in the crack of light. 'Time for a coffee, a Guatemalan?'

'One last cup. Thanks, Lorna.'

# 14

Ella was wheeled into her father's adapted van and strapped in. She sat behind him at the wheel and had a clear view in front and at the side of the vehicle. They set off for Brodick and the ferry to Ardrossan.

Permission was given for Rory to stay in the van with his daughter for the duration of the sailing. An hour later they docked and drove off into Ayrshire's mainland. As the van continued north, their minds were distracted.

'Dad, if the operation goes wrong, what will happen?'

Rory gripped the steering wheel. 'I'll stay with you and see you home safely, darling.'

Ella's question had not been answered to her satisfaction. It showed in her crinkled face. 'Dad, might I die in the hospital?'

Rory's throat tightened. In the moment's silence which followed he gathered his thoughts. 'We all die. Not many die 100 years old but some do. Some, in their early twenties die in car accidents. Whole families are killed in air crashes too. That's why we take each day as it comes,' he said feeling he had given an appropriate response.

'If I die, I will always love you.'

Rory smiled at Ella taking his eyes off the road momentarily. 'And I love you more than all the granules of sand on the island.' And they laughed. 'But darling these surgeons know what they are doing. You are one of the oldest patients they will have had in the Sick Children's hospital at Yorkhill but their experience will be immense. If I was in doubt, I'd not have signed the permission required for the operation.'

Ella's lips smiled. She patted her father's shoulder lightly in a moment of gratitude.

Much to his pleasant surprise, the hospital gave Rory a bed in the wing. He had not expected that but was told the patients were often very much younger and their recovery was aided by family members being nearby. This pleased Ella immensely.

The operation would be at 8.30 am the following morning. They quickly settled in their new surroundings. Mr. Ian Young, the surgeon, called to see them.

'So this is Ella. I'm very pleased to meet you,' he said stepping forward to shake her hand. Ella was taken aback and found she had no reply, but a smile nevertheless emerged.

'Mr. Murdoch, I presume?'

'Yes, Ella's father.'

'You will both be brought a meal soon so I had better not keep you long. Tomorrow you will have no breakfast. Ella. So eat up this evening,' he laughed. 'You, Mr. Murdoch of course, will have breakfast.'

Rory smiled.

'Ella you will be taken on a trolley to the theatre and when you get there, you will meet the anaesthetist. She will hold your hand and give you a jab. I promise you won't feel a thing. Then she'll ask you to count down from 10. Now that's easy isn't it?'

'Yes, very easy,' said Ella.

'I bet you won't get to 4,' he laughed. Ella looked confused.

'The anaesthetic will have you dreaming before you get to the last few numbers,' said Rory holding his daughter's right hand.

'And that's really all there is because when you wake up, you will be back in this room and your father will be here to welcome you. Now, do you have any questions?

'Er...no. I don't,' said Ella.

'Mr. Murdoch?'

'How long will the operation take?'

'I wish I had an answer for you. Sometimes two hours sometimes almost four. It could take anytime between these estimates.'

'The same operation?' he queried.

'Yes, the same operation.'

A trolley was heard approaching.

'Well, it's almost time for home and a meal for me too,' said Mr. Young.

The trolley entered the room, and a table was positioned over Ella's bed. Ella's eyes lit up to see fish fingers and chips with a couple of sprigs of broccoli.

As the auxiliary poured some orange juice into a cup, the surgeon left the room then turned around. Out of sight of Ella, he pointed at Rory and curled his finger.

'Back in a moment Ella,' he said and made for the corridor.

Mr. Young lowered his voice. 'This is not the easiest of operations. When things go wrong it takes longer. There are many nerve endings we must avoid but let me assure you we will do our utmost to get everything right.'

He patted Rory's elbow but Rory was concentrating on what the surgeon had told him.

'Till tomorrow, good night Mr. Murdoch.'

'Er...good night.'

Outside on the Glasgow streets, the night was dreich and dismal. Not heavy rain but the penetrating drizzle for which the city is famed. That night, as the city lights peered weakly into the ward Rory turned in his sleep and saw his daughter sleep soundly. He closed his eyes and the noise of the corridor vanished. The next time he opened them there was a shaft of light in the room. He looked at his watch. It was already 6 am at the hospital was alive once more at work.

Rory was served breakfast. Ella watched him eat. He sat on Ella's bed with a cup of tea, reassuring her that in many hospitals, patients were getting ready to have their operations too.

'But this is my operation,' said an insightful Ella and Rory agreed with a nod.

Half an hour later the trolley appeared by her bedside and Ella was gingerly slid onto it. With a wave of her arm, she set off, with Rory holding a fixed smile as he waved to his daughter, wishing for her an eventless operation.

Rory looked out of the window. He saw cars like matchbox vehicles travelling in either direction overtaking buses which were making their designated stops to pick up umbrella folding passengers. Then he heard some movement behind him. A volunteer was pushing around a trolley of crisps, drinks, sweeties, and newspapers. Rory raised his arm and the woman stopped.

'Daily Express, please.'

The lady folded the paper in one hand and took Rory's money in the other.

'Parent?' she asked.

Rory nodded taken aback. 'Yes, my daughter...' but his response faded.

'Many go out for a walk to pass the time. There's a park not too far away,' she said pointing in its general direction.

'Perhaps not yet,' Rory replied as the rain began to dribble down the window.

She laughed. 'Oh, of course not. But this is Glasgow. It will soon dry up. You know four seasons in a day, keeps us on our toes,' she giggled, and then she twirled around and left the room.

Rory sat down to read his paper. Although the pages turned over at a steady rate, he absorbed the photo information. He soon got to the crossword. He took out his pen, folded the paper appropriately, and began to tax his mind.

The coffee/tea urn was next to pass his door and Rory took the opportunity to recapture his office routine. As he stirred in the sugar in his paper cup, his mind turned to the unconscious daughter. He could do nothing to comfort her. He needed to recharge his batteries. The coffee was not Guatemalan, so he needed some other stimulant.

He looked out of the window and true to the volunteer's word, the weather was changing. Patches of blue sky slowly became visible and rain no longer ran down the windowpane. Rory put down his paper, gulped the last two mouthfuls of coffee then fastened his anorak and went for a walk.

Glasgow was humid, yet the cool wind was refreshing. The pedestrians, although smiles were on their faces, passed by like soldiers heading for battle in offices, vehicles, or shops. This was so unlike peaceful Arran.

Rory found the park, an oasis in the middle of the city and surprisingly quiet. Mothers with prams sauntered by and dogs on leads sniffed other dogs, making conversation with their owners compulsory. Glasgow the friendly city, that smiles better, was living up to its character.

Rory found a green metal seat and sat down to contemplate his life. Had he really overstepped the mark at work? Was that the end of his professional police career? How would the Police Federation react? Ah yes, an unfair dismissal was the procedure. But he'd have to be certain of success.

He returned to the ward after an hour and a half in the open air. Ella was not back in the room yet. He completed the crossword and began to read the main news in greater detail.

Then Ella's trolley entered the room. She was still unconscious. The nurse in attendance turned towards Rory. 'Try not to waken her. Let her come-to, in her own time.'

Rory nodded. 'The operation went well?' he had to ask in a whisper.

The nurse turned towards Rory. 'The operation took longer than expected. But she'll be fine. The surgeon will come in to see you soon.'

Rory sighed with relief. He looked at his daughter just as she opened her mouth and yawned. He felt proud of her and hoped the operation would improve her life significantly.

Mr. Young knocked on the door. He entered and looked at Ella. Then he turned towards Rory. 'Quite a fighter is Ella. She's come through a lot this morning. The shunt seemed reluctant to settle. That caused us problems. But that's all done and dusted. She will be fine,' he said then looked at his watch. 'Gosh, I see it's almost afternoon already.'

'Yes, I took a walk in the park,' Rory replied nervously.

Mr. Young smiled in a distracted manner. His mind had moved on. 'Do you have a carer for Ella?'

'Yes, but I'm now at home so I might not need her so much.'

Mr. Young looked at Rory. 'Did you take early retirement?'

Rory wondered how relevant his questioning was. 'Yes, I did,' he lied uncomfortably.

'I wish more in your situation would do too. There's nothing like care from the family,' he suggested. 'Ella will take a few days to recover. She will stretch her back slowly. The shunt has got to feel comfortable. Your SB nurse will let us know if there is a problem. But the operation is over, and she will sit slightly straighter. She will feel the benefit.'

There was a moment of silent reflection. 'When can I take her home?'

The surgeon looked at Ella and saw she was coming around. 'She'll be speaking soon. Then she'll, er. I mean, you'll both get some lunch and if that goes down well, then I guess you will be leaving us around 3 pm. How does that suit you?'

'Yes, that's fine. I'll call Ardrossan and book the 6:30 pm sailing home.'

They caught the early evening sailing and just over the hour they were driving south to Whiting Bay and home. Ella felt good and was anxious to show how much more straight she could be. Rory hugged her.

'You're going to be just fine,' he said landing a kiss on her cheek.

The following morning as the last spoonful of cereal was swallowed, the telephone rang. It was Lorna.

'Hi, all well? How is Ella?'

'Ella's fighting fit. The operation was a success, thank you.'

'Good. ...Rory, I'm phoning you because there's a letter for you.'

'You mean confirmation from the D.I., I suppose?'

'No actually. I think you should drop in to collect it, it's from Belgium.'

'Belgium? It's for me? Are you sure?'

'Well, I think so. It's addressed to Mr. Murdock.'

'Murdock? Dock, are you sure?

'Well they spelled Murdoch with a 'K.' They gave Rory three 'Rs' and they promoted you to sergeant, but it's definitely a Belgian envelope for you.'

'God knows how they got my name. Rorry with two 'R's indeed. Sounds like a hoax. I'll be down soon.'

Belgium, Rory pondered. He'd never been there. But, he supposed, they had made a good go at getting his name right.

After morning tea and toast, getting Ella dressed and sitting up on her special chair, Rory excused himself and made for the police station.

'Good morning, Lorna. This is unusual. I'm meant to have left this place. Now you bring me back for a letter.'

'Here it is,' she said handing the brown envelope over. 'I'll bring you a coffee. Go back to your room and read it. Perhaps it's a billet-doux from a European admirer?'

'Lorna. I assure you that is most unlikely.'

'Oh there's a letter from Nelson too, I opened it when you were in Glasgow.'

Rory entered his old room. Nothing had changed. He sat down feeling he was still at work. Nelson's letter was one of support. He'd stand up for him if Rory went for unfair dismissal. And he was compiling D.I. Grant's instructions, noting the ones showing his over authoritarian voice. Rory smiled. He had at least one supporter.

He lifted the Belgian letter to see it franked Charleroi sur Sambre. He admired the stamp it bore. French-speaking Walloon country in the south he remembered. He lifted the atlas from the bookcase. He took his magnifying glass from his drawer and found the town quite near the French border. He sliced open the Belgian letter and pulled out the folded sheets. He opened them. He looked at them. They were written all in French.

*Je vous écris en tant que gouverneur adjoint de la prison de Charleroi. Nous avons un prisonnier nommé Eric Lacroix. Il purge une peine de 18 ans après avoir été reconnu coupable du crime de traite.*

*Il a informé son compagnon de cellule, Guillaume Baratchart, qu'il avait enterré une jeune fille sur Arran en Écosse, dans un champ il y a environ deux ans auparavant. Apparemment parce qu'elle refusait de se prostituer et d'accepter un travail organisé pour elle à Gourock dans une boutique d'ongles. C'était une fille de Syrie.*

*Je ne sais pas si vous étudiez toujours qui elle est, mais je pense que ces informations vous seront utiles. N'hésitez pas à me répondre si vous souhaitez plus d'informations.*

The text was double-Dutch to Rory. The sciences and art were his favourite school subjects and foreign languages were an anathema to him. He returned the letter to its envelope and stood up. He noticed his Busy Lizzie had been neglected so he lifted the pot and placed it in a shopping bag he had with him.

'Well, did she propose?' Lorna asked with a wink as he left his room.

'It was from the assistant Governor of the Charleroi prison.'

'Oh, so if you don't mind me asking, what was he saying?'

'I wish I could tell you,' he replied.

'Ah top secret, I suspect. Perhaps asking you to join Interpol?'

'Yes, very secret. It's in French.'

On Rory's return home he wasted no time watered his Busy Lizzie, he placed it on the kitchen window sill then told his daughter about his French letter. There was a hesitation and then they both laughed. 'I mean Belgian letter, in French,' he said surprised at her knowledge of such a risqué joke.

Rory then remembered his neighbour next but one was a secondary school teacher of French. He looked at his watch. Lunch-time. That would give him some thought about how to proceed with it. He read the letter over and over and concluded it mentioned two names and they both seemed to be in custody at the prison and Arran was mentioned.

But he needed to have the exact translation, to make sense of what was written.

At 5 pm he telephoned Wendy. 'Hi, Rory here. I've got a letter written in French. I wonder if you would translate it for me.'

'Is it a work letter?'

'Yes, as a matter of fact, it is?'

'Then presumably you will have to kill me once it's translated?'

Rory laughed. 'I might kill you if you talked about it. I'm joking. But I'd appreciate it if you could translate it. It has two pages only,' he laughed to reassure her.

'I suppose there's no time like the present. I've not started to make the evening meal.'

'I'm on my way.' Rory found a pen and a notebook. He was prepared.


Wendy's lounge had a grand view of the bay. Rory stood to admire the view. He had a few trees which had grown tall making his own view restricted.

Wendy closed the lounge door and stretched out her hand. Rory delivered the brown envelope to her.

She read it through first. 'It's an interesting letter you have here.'

'Yes, I am sure it is.'

'Looks like you have found the Blackwaterfoot murderer,' she said with high eyebrows. 'Are you ready to write down the translation?'

Rory opened his notebook to a blank page. He looked up at her, smiled with satisfaction over her remark and nodded. He was more than ready to hear what the Belgian Governor had written.

'Well it's from Charleroi prison.'

'The governor, that much I know.'

'It goes on....

*I am writing to you as deputy governor of Charleroi prison. We have a prisoner here named Eric Lacroix. He is serving an 18-year sentence after being convicted of the crime of trafficking.*

*He informed his cellmate, Guillaume Baratchart, that he had buried a young girl on Arran in Scotland, in a field about two years earlier. Apparently, because she refused to prostitute herself and to accept work in a nail shop organized for her in Gourock. She was a girl from Syria.*

*I don't know if you are still studying this case or who she is but I think you will find this information useful. Do not hesitate to contact me if you want more information.*

'Have you got all that?'

'Word for word. That's great. How can I thank you enough?'

'Nonsense, it's my bread and butter. I'm more than happy to help a neighbour. After all, if I commit an offence, I'd come straight to you and remind you of this job successfully completed,' she said running her fingers backwards through her brown hair and laughing.

After making the evening meal then washing up, Rory went over the translation once more. Yes, he knew he had the murderer. Tomorrow morning he'd have to contact the D.I.

# 15

At 9.30 am the following morning as Ella listened to West Sound Radio, Rory phoned D.I. Grant.

'Good morning Mr. Grant,'

'Is that you Murdoch?'

'Yes, it is.'

'Then it's D.I. Grant, to you.'

'Sorry, sir. How is the search for Jim Randall going?'

'You Rory are suspended. I have nothing to tell you about Mr. Randall. In fact, I don't need to speak to you.'

'Maybe not, but I have news for you. I have resolved the mur...'

D.I. Grant was not in the mood to hear his good news. He cut Rory off.

Rory shook his head. He took no time at all to dial Nelson. This time he got down to the matter, indeed the murder at hand.

'Hi, you will never guess. The murder down at Blackwaterfoot is solved.'

'But Rory, we know Randall killed his stepdaughter. That's hardly in doubt.'

'No, listen. Remember there were two murders at Blackwaterfoot? The first one, the skeleton, I know who did it.'

Out of sight, Nelson sat down to understand what his former colleague was saying. 'Are you sure?'

'Yes, he's a Belgian called Eric Lacroix. He is a trafficker and is in prison in Charleroi.'

'Rory are you really sure?'

'I am as sure as night follows day.'

'How err... why?'

'A Belgian prison governor wrote to me,' Rory tried to clarify. 'Well, assistant governor but yes, in Belgium. He explained the murder conversation between two prisoners to me,' said Rory feeling great about his unexpected news.

'Then you'd better tell D.I. Grant.'

Rory gave a huge lung full sigh. 'No, I want you to tell him.'

'It was you who made the link. It would be good for your defence if it came from you.'

'It is already on my mind, Nelson. I was telling him when he put the phone down on me. That man is just baiting me.'

There was a silence as Nelson ordered his many thoughts. 'Then I'll do that right away for you. Expect a phone call soon. He's bound to take over again, and not to mention, probably take all the credit for it as well.'

Indeed, he could expect a call soon but instead, he telephoned forensic scientist Dr. Jane Dunbar and told her the good news. She was thrilled it had led to the murderer as she felt sure it would be unsolvable. Before he ended the telephone call, he asked what she thought of D.I. Grant.

'That man!' she yelled. 'He's got no feelings. He's a bully and I'm just glad I am not usually on his territory. But am I speaking out of turn?'

Rory grabbed his hair and pulled it. His smile was as wide as the Brodick esplanade. 'No Jane. What you have said is music to my ears.' Without a further word he put the phone down and contemplated a morning coffee. Instead, he read the Go Girl magazine to Ella.

He was in the middle of a story when the phone rang. How would he find the D.I.? Apologetic perhaps? No, that was not in his make-up. He lifted the phone.

'Is that Rory?' the voice asked. Rory could not put a finger on whom it might be. 'Yes,' he replied cautiously.

'Hi, Tony Cohen here, Police Federation secretary. I hear you have been suspended. We want to support you. Will you want to dispute your situation, or will you ...er...take early retirement?'

'Yes, I do feel D.I. Grant has been hard on me. And I'm not thinking of retirement yet.'

'That's what we like to hear. It's not the first time he's been warned. This time I hope we have enough rope to hang him.'

'A bit severe don't you think?

'Just a saying, but I hope it will be a demotion if not a dismissal. Do you have any supporters?'

'Yes, a few.'

'And who are they?'

'My secretary Lorna in Whiting Bay, Nelson in Lochranza and Jane er...Dr. Jane Dunbar at Pitt Street, the forensic scientist.'

'A good start. I'll get statements from them first. Meantime, relax. I'll be in touch later.'

'Great, that's a relief,' Rory said replacing the handset then punching the air.

'Have I read enough, yet?'

Ella replied with a nod and sleepy eyes.

'Then I'll get my paper now.' He put on his jacket and made for the newsagents. The sun was up and despite a gentle breeze; there were no clouds so he knew Ella could sit out in the garden on his return if she wasn't sleeping. He bought his paper and sauntered home without any significant care in his world. On his return home, he was brought down to earth.

'Dad, the telephone has been ringing.'

'Oh, don't worry. If it's important they'll phone again.' Rory had hardly finished replying to his daughter when the phone did ring again.

'Hello,' he responded.

'Where the hell were you? D.I. Grant here.'

'That's not your concern. I was out. Have you been phoning me?'

'Listen Nelson tells me you have the name of the murderer of the skeleton.'

'That's right. I was trying to tell you that when you cut me off,' he said pulling a chair behind him to sit down.

'Don't procrastinate. Where is he? We've got to arrest him immediately!'

Rory laughed realising Nelson had not given him the full story. 'He's safe where he is. There's no rush required.'

'That's not for you to decide. Remember you are Mr. Joe Public right now.'

'As I said, he's safe. He's in prison already for trafficking.'

'Murder is much worse than trafficking. Which prison? He'll have to be interviewed. I'll have to arrange that. God, you make life so difficult for me at times, Mr. Murdoch.'

'He's in Belgium. In Charleroi prison.'

There was a moment's silence as Grant thought the situation through. Rory heard his heavy breathing and the tapping of his pen.

'And how the hell did you find that out?'

'The prison assistant governor wrote to me.'

'He wrote to you? Then send me the letter, promptly.'

'Delighted to do so. Anything to catch this murderer,' said Rory recalling the original text was in French.

'By the way, when did you get the letter?'

'The other day.'

'After you were suspended?'

'Now you mention it, yes it was. But the Governor didn't know that.'

The phone went dead.

Rory opened his lounge desk and produced a white envelope. He placed the Belgian letter in it and opened a small drawer where he kept stamps. He lifted a stamp, saw it was first class, and rejected it. He took out a second class stamp and fixed it to the envelope. He hollered through to Ella.

'Just popping out to post a letter, darling.'

There was no reply. He looked into the kitchen where she was slumped in her chair fast asleep. He thought about propping her up but felt it had been a tiring time for her, so he left her to sleep.

He closed the door silently and set off along the pavement tapping the letter on his leg, to a beat of 'it's in French, it's in French' and imagining the D.I. struggling to read the letter.

# 16

An envelope passed through the front door flap like a descending glider and Flop the spaniel barked. It aroused Ella's attention.

'Mail, Dad.'

Rory sauntered through and found the official-looking envelope being guarded by Flop. He lifted it up and saw the Police insignia on the rear flap of the envelope. He took it to the kitchen where a bread knife sliced the missive open. It was from the Police Federation. Rory scanned the lines. It had been sent by Tony Cohen, the Police Federation secretary, and invited Rory to attend a hearing to be held, taking account of Rory's domestic situation, at the rear of the Public Hall in Brodick, the following week. Tony mentioned that the rooms had been privately booked. Rory's supporters were listed whereas D.I. Sammy Grant had yet to produce his witnesses.

Over the next week, Rory attended to his garden and took Ella out for runs in his car. She was almost a new girl as she stood taller and kept that poise as long as she could. Two days before the hearing Rory received a call quite out of the blue.

'Hello, Mr. Murdoch. I'm Fiona Black the Ayr Procurator Fiscal. I thought I'd tell you that today I lodged an extradition warrant for Eric Lacroix and requested the police in Charleroi to obtain a full statement from his cellmate Guillaume Baratchart.'

'Er...how did you get my number?' he asked as what she had been saying wriggled around in his mind.

'Your secretary at the police station gave it to me.'

'But didn't you know I am suspended? I'm not a policeman now.'

'You may not be a policeman now Mr. Murdoch, but you are one of my main witnesses.'

'You mean because I received the information from Belgium?'

'Yes, and were you not the officer who was first on the scene of the skeleton?'

'Yes, I suppose I was,' Rory said scratching the back of his head.

'May I ask what led to your suspension? I'll keep it confidential, I promise. But it's best I know, in case you are discredited as a witness.'

'Well, it's a long story but whatever caused it, I don't really know but D.I. Grant had it in for me right from the start.'

'D.I. Sammy Grant?'

'Yes, you know him?'

'Of course, I do. He is a regular police witness in the court here in Ayr. Not the brightest of sparks.'

'Not the brightest...' Rory began with a grin exposing a row of filling-free teeth, '...exactly what do you mean?'

'Well, it's not just me. All my fiscal colleagues have a poor view of him. He's often ill-prepared for court and when he's not familiar with the case, he's a tongue-wagging fantasist,' she said, and her annoyance was unmistakable over the phone.'

'Fiona, could I get you and your staff to prepare a statement about his court failings?'

'If it helps your case, I'd be delighted to do that.'

'That's great. Can you send it to the Police Federation secretary?'

'You mean Tony Cohen?' she asked.

'Yes, you know him?

'Know him? You bet. He's my sister's husband.'

'Your brother-in-law?'

'Yes indeed, in-law as you say.'

Rory replaced the handset and gave out a loud shout.

'What's up, Dad? Are you all right?'

'Ella, my case is getting stronger.'

# 17

Rory was up at the crack of dawn. He had ironed his shirt the night before and polished his black shoes. After having a soapy shower, he got Ella dressed. She knew this was an important day for her father.

An hour later Ella's day carer arrived, and she was quick to tell her that her father was going to an important meeting, but Hazel did not pursue the conversation, not knowing if Ella should have mentioned it in the first place. Hazel had already heard through the local grapevine that there would be a winner and a loser at the meeting and a Constable facing a D.I. was like David facing Goliath. Or could it be the hare and the tortoise? She gave it no more thought and filled the washing bowl with soapy hot water to clean the breakfast dishes.

Rory set off to Brodick and parked on Manse Road near the Public Hall. He filled his lungs with the sea air and walked down the esplanade. He saw the Calmac ferry approach the quay and knew the mainland contingent would be on that boat.

Rory arrived at the Public Hall and waited anxiously for proceedings to start. At 10 am on the dot he was invited into the back room. He saw Assistant Chief Constable Ian McDonald in the chair and sitting at the table was Tony Cohen who smiled as Rory entered. D.I. Sammy Grant was already seated looking smart in his uniform with brown leather gloves on his lap.

As soon as the Assistant Chief Constable spoke, Rory recognised an island highlander, possibly a

Lewis man. But he put that thought to one side and concentrated on what he had to say.

After laying before them the ground-rules of the hearing, he invited D.I. Grant to put his case forward.

'Certainly, sir, I certainly will. Constable Murdoch is a pain in my arse. I have ...'

'Mr. Grant, I will dismiss this case immediately if you proceed in that derogatory tone and manner. You have been warned. Now continue please,' said the ACC.

Sammy Grant looked over at Rory briefly, but he stared straight ahead.

'Mr. Murdoch is slow; he has the lowest conviction rate in the country. He...'

Rory's eyebrows creased and he mouthed the word 'country.'

The ACC was quick off the mark. 'And Mr. Grant if Mr. Murdoch has the lowest conviction rate in the country, who is next lowest and who is the highest?'

Mr. Grant smiled at the table before him. 'I suspect I will be one with the highest rate of convictions but I have no idea who is second lowest.'

'Then if you have no idea who is second lowest and only a suspicion that you have the highest, I suspect you cannot claim Mr. Murdoch to have the lowest of Arran and Ayrshire. You are not comparing like with like appropriately. You may have a high rate of charging, I accept, but what's your conviction rate? Percentage wise, Mr Grant?'

'As I was saying...'

'No, Mr. Grant. I asked a question. It's an answer I expect.'

The ACC focussed his eyes on the D.I. and in the silence which followed Sammy Grant realised he had few friends around the table.

'Your conviction percentages seem to have departed your mind. So, carry on then, what other failings do you see in Mr. Murdoch?'

Mr. Grant pulled at his shirt cuffs as he continued his case. 'Mr. Murdoch is argumentative; he doesn't take commands straight away. He seems to regurgitate my orders first.'

'Examples please.'

'Yes, there are a few. At the scene of the first murder, the skeleton, he seemed ill at ease, not sure of what he was doing. I did not get his full co-operation. At Lochranza he was unwilling to take my very clear order.'

'Which was?'

Sammy Grant had dug a hole for himself. He realised the weakness of his case. Vagueness was his solution. 'It was about timing. I told Murdoch to return the next day to take into custody and question Jim Randall. Murdoch had had a long day. I wanted him to be fresh.'

'Mr. Grant, an officer making an arrest is never tired. In fact, from what I understand of the case, your instruction led to a murder and a missing suspect,' said the mild-mannered but firm highland ACC. 'What are your other complaints?'

'Well too many to record at the drop of a hat,' he said turning red at the neck.

'I would have thought you would have allotted some time to record Mr. Murdoch's failings. I certainly have the time to hear them, Mr. Grant.'

'We just don't get on. I can't work with him in my team. We are not suited. I suppose that's the basis of my complaint. Insubordination due to incompatibility,' he said folding his arms defensively. 'We need to keep apart.'

'And that is your case?'

Grant pursed his lips and nodded. 'Yes sir.'

Rory was on edge but confident in what he would say when his time came.

AAC McDonald surprised Rory.

'I'd like twenty minutes. I have some reports to read and reflect on. Gentlemen we shall adjourn for a short break.

Rory stood up as did Sammy. They caught each other's eye. Rory reached the door first and waved his senior through. Sammy left the room without expressing any gratitude for the gesture. Before Rory shut the door, he looked up at the table. The ACC smiled then lowered his eyes to the open pages of reports. Was he preparing his decision without his participation? Surely not.

Rory stood at the front door of the hall looking out over the car park while Sammy Grant had lit a cigarette. He watched as the blue-grey smoke rose and disappeared like a conjuror's trick. Then he went over to his car and sat in the driver's seat. He knew there would be only one decision. Either he would be re-instated to fight Sammy Grant again one day or he would be disciplined and asked to leave the force. That would give Grant too much satisfaction, but he felt he could attend to his daughter's needs more readily, although he accepted Ella's carer was a godsend. He felt the decision could go either way. It depended on what the ACC made of the defence he was about to deliver.

From the hall step the ACC's secretary waved Rory in and by the time he entered, Sammy Grant was seated already.

'Gentlemen, I have reached my conclusion and will deliver it in silence.'

Rory's face was contorted, and the ACC saw it. 'There is no need for you to present any evidence, Mr. Murdoch.'

What did that mean? Was he giving Rory grounds to appeal? He listened intently to the ACC.

'This is a case of one officer working in a busy built-up largely deprived Ayrshire conurbation. The towns of Saltcoats, Ardrossan, Irvine, and Kilmarnock, constitute a very busy patch indeed, while another officer works on a quiet island where practically everyone knows each other, and very little crime is committed. Targets are meaningless in such a small community. Inevitably there would be envy. But the roles were reversed and murders came to Arran in ongoing cases and so the stage was set for confrontation.'

Sammy Grant pursed his lips feeling satisfied that the ACC had recognised he had a busier job to do on the mainland. Rory meanwhile sat with his mouth partly open and very dry, still listening to every word.

'Had that been the only evidence I had, I'd encourage you to shake hands and get on with the work. But there's more to this case.'

Rory's head was raised as he concentrated on this unexpected development. Sammy Grant fidgeted in his seat uncomfortably.

'Firstly, I have read Dr. Jane Dunbar's report. It does not make good reading. Dr. Dunbar is an experienced highly qualified forensic scientist. She has had a few run-ins with you, Mr. Grant. Scientists don't take instructions on how they do their work. Then I have Constable Colin Nelson's report. He finds you bombastic, bullying, and controlling. Fiona Black the fiscal says you come to court unprepared, she's lost a couple of cases because the jury was misled, by you. Her report is signed by three other fiscals in support of her report.' The ACC shook his head without his eyes leaving the reports. Then he looked up at D.I. Grant. 'What are your hobbies?'

D.I. Grant took a deep satisfying breath. The subject had changed at last.

'Well, I like to get a bit of loch fishing done and climbing some hills at the weekend. Re-energizing myself for each new week at work. That's how I cope in a busy patch,' he declared with an air of self-satisfaction.

'I see. And fishing, what is your favourite fly. Which one gets the trout?'

D.I. Grant was on familiar territory now. What was more, the ACC was a fisherman too it seemed. They had something in common and that augured well he thought.

'I prefer the Hare & Copper, or the Red Eyed Damsel, yes that's my favourite,' he said sitting back on equal terms with the ACC. He turned to give Rory a sly look.

'Tried the Mustard Caddis or the...Woolly Bugger?' the ACC asked with a glance over to Rory as if to imply he was getting along with the D.I.

'No, but the Caddis, I've tried. It has a dark head and a lighter feather. Good for the peat lochs,' said Grant with a satisfying smile.

Rory was dismayed by the conversation.

The ACC ended the pastime chat. The silence lasted at least eight seconds. He was preparing to sum up and Rory was right. His future depended on every word he was about to hear now. He was as alert as the hare noticing an eagle fly above.

'Gentlemen, I have heard enough and read from reports to draw this conclusion. D.I. Grant, I wish you to undergo an anger management course. Thereafter, I will transfer you to the island of Jura. It's a one policeman post with the occasional call from Islay to assist. Accordingly, you are demoted to the rank of constable. On Jura, you will be able to fish some well-stocked lochs and of course, the Paps of Jura offers some spectacular views to enhance your climbing skills. That is my decision. The alternative is for you to take early retirement.'

The ACC looked up at Grant. He was looking for an initial response.

Grant was wide-mouthed and in shock. 'But... I've.... not yet done my....thirty years,' he said in a stuttering and trembling voice.

'That is why Police Scotland is giving you the opportunity to take this post, which was recently made available, through retirement. Of course, you have the right to appeal against my decision. However, I stress the anger management course will be a prerequisite prior to your engagement on Jura.'

The atmosphere remained tense. Rory's hands were clasped so tightly under the table that they turned white, starved of blood. His face was equally pallid.

'Mr. Murdoch,' the ACC said and then suspended his next sentence for five seconds giving Rory several palpitations. 'You have had twenty-eight years of service is that not so?'

Rory got to his feet. 'Yes, er.... just a little over that,' he said with a dry mouth.

'Of course, and you are a witness in the trial of Eric Lacroix?'

'Yes sir, I will be.'

'And a prime witness in the case of Jim Randall?'

'Yes. As soon as he is apprehended that case will proceed at the High Court where I will indeed be a main witness.'

'Then I wish you luck in these pursuits. Your suspension is over. And I give you this ruling. You will return to Lamlash, as a sergeant, and take responsibility for the pending murder trials. Or, and I respect you will take cognisance of your circumstances at home, retire on full pay. Mr. Murdoch, the choice is yours. You may wish more time to think about it,'

Rory could hardly believe what options he was being told. Promotion, control of three murder cases, or retirement? Perhaps retirement in a few years but he felt able to follow through the murder cases. And Ella had her carers when he was at work. He stood to give the ACC his response.

'You have given me two stark choices. My daughter's health is a concern but her recent operation has given her a new lease of life. She gets on well with her carer. I can handle my responsibilities both at home and at work.'

He took a deep breath then smiled at the ACC. 'Even being in Ayr for both trials, I accept your offer to resume my police career, as sergeant at Lamlash.'

Rory's face was now solemn. He turned towards his former D.I. and looked at him. 'However, I wish Constable Grant well in his new assignment on Jura. He may not have as many murders as we have had on Arran recently but sheep rustling, raptor egg-stealing, and health and safety infringements due to farmer's slurry being left to infiltrate streams then rivers have come my way. Rural policing provides an interesting caseload, I am sure you will find that too. Of course, there will be far fewer Breach of the Peace cases. Much more interesting files will come your way, I know. But with your experience of being a D.I., I am sure you can put that to good use, even though you will be working on your own.'

Rory sat down. He had gone over the mark somewhat in praising Grant, but he had not been stopped by the ACC. Indeed, he had possibly taken the words out of his mouth.

'You have both made your choices. If you in the coming days decide it was a decision made in haste, then I remind you the right of appeal extends to three weeks. That is the end of this hearing. The matters are now closed.'

With these short sentences, ACC Ian McDonald stood, gathered his papers into a folder, and left the room. Rory turned to Grant and extended his hand as an act of conclusion, but Constable Sammy Grant turned the other way and left the room. Rory sat down once more and placed his head in his hands. He thought through the hearing then he remembered the Co-op was still open and a bottle of red wine would form part of that night's meal.

# 18

Lorna was delighted to hear that Rory was back to work and so was Nelson. Lorna decked his room with a vase of roses and when he arrived at work, met him with a hug.

'I enjoyed the break to some extent and the timing of Ella's surgery was good. But the worry was an early retirement with a reduced pension. That's all in the past now and it's great to be back,' said Rory as Lorna put water in the kettle.

'There's another Belgian letter for you. You'll need a coffee to get the gist of that. I'll bring the mail through, Sergeant, with your usual coffee.'

'No need to call me anything but Rory,' he smiled as he kicked the door open and entered his office.

Thoughts of contacting his neighbour Wendy again passed through his mind, as he waited for his coffee to percolate. That would please him. He felt he got on well with her. When the mail arrived, he flipped through the lot in one hand and found the larger foreign envelope at the bottom. He could not resist having a first glance at it. Perhaps he could interpret a few words, now that he had both French and English translations of the previous letter.

He pulled the two pages from the envelope and opened them up to see the text was in English. He noticed the letter had been written by a Commissioner of Police. His English was understandable if somewhat antiquated.

*Dear Mr. Murdoch,*

*Greetings from the Charleroi.*

    *I hope you are to be well. We have had a letter of correspondence from your Procurator Fiscal, Miss Fiona Black. Her letter enclosed a letter of instruction to deliver Mr. Eric Lacroix to the court at Ayr to face the charge of Murder of a Syrian youth. May I request information as to where this man is to be detained until he comes to the court? This is my main objective in writing to you.*
    *I look forward to hearings of your advice.*

*Respectfully written*

*I am your servant*

*Jules Ives*

Rory put the letter to one side, took a sip of his hot coffee then sprung open his telephone address book and landed at K. He lifted the receiver and telephoned the Governor of Kilmarnock prison.

'Mr. Kerr? This is Constable Murdoch at Lamlash. Oh er.... sorry I'm actually Sergeant Murdoch now,' he said, feeling stupid and unprofessional in forgetting his rank.

'Congratulations on your promotion,' Mr Kerr responded.

Rory decided not to tell him how his promotion came about, it would be too complicated. 'I have a prisoner in Belgium who is to appear at Ayr sheriff court. Can you accommodate him?'

'Is that not D.I. Grant who usually informs me of foreign prisoners?'

Rory bit his lip. 'D.I. Grant is no longer in Ayrshire....,' he began, but he was interrupted.

'Ah Police Scotland promoted him to Glasgow, I presume?'

'No, far from that reality. He has been reduced in rank and farmed out to Jura as Constable Sammy Grant.'

There was a pause. 'Well, you know, I'm not really surprised somehow. He wasn't the most popular of policemen around here. But that's none of my business.'

'Anyway, is there a bed in Kilmarnock prison when he comes over?'

'No, we don't really have beds and cells. We are run on behalf of the Scottish Prison Service by Serco and we have suites. It's a relatively new prison opened in 1999 with modern concepts,' Mr. Kerr said in a moment of pride.

'A suite then?'

'When is the trial date?'

'In two weeks.'

'So how will he arrive?'

'I presume they will fly him to Prestwick.'

'Well, when you confirm the flight, I'll send a van to the airport to collect him.'

'Excellent.'

'Oh, and I should have asked earlier, what offence is he serving prison for in Belgium.'

'Trafficking offence.'

'A traffic offence? My, there must have been something else to gain a prison sentence,' he said with incredulity.

Rory pouted his lips. Mr. Kerr had not heard him correctly. 'No, trafficking people.'

'Ah, of course. We've not had one of those yet. So, what's the case in Ayr?'

'Murder.'

There was a pause. 'That skeleton in the field by any chance, which that the bull discovered?'

'So, you know about the case?'

'Of course, it was all over the papers. A bull finding a body. The press went to town on that one, I can assure you.'

When Eric Lacroix arrived in Ayrshire, he was appointed Mark Dykes as his QC. He was assisted by Mr. Des Delaney. Both went to the prison to meet Lacroix and prepared their case. This was not good news for Rory. Des Delaney had a record of being sarcastic, arrogant, and certainly did not suffer fools gladly. But he was not High court material, yet. This was Fiona Black's view too. Fiona meanwhile assisted Bill Smith QC.

At last, the case was called within Ayr sheriff court. The High Court of Judiciary sat there to determine this case and Lord McEwan took his seat. Eric Lacroix looked continental somehow. Perhaps it was his string beard that looped around his chin or his rainbow spectacle legs but whatever it was, he did not look local. Indeed, an interpreter sat beside him to translate any phrase or saying he could not follow. However, as an international trafficker, Lacroix spoke four European languages efficiently, according to the Belgian police. Rory felt the presence of an interpreter was a plot tantamount to an appeal claiming his client would not have a fair trial because he could not fully understand the proceedings. Mr. Delaney would have surely suggested this to Mr. Dykes QC.

Mr. Bill Smith QC rose to cite the charge for the prosecution.

'On a date unknown within the past two years, you did kill and deposit the body of an unknown Syrian woman in a field near Blackwaterfoot on the island of Arran.'

Lord McEwan asked Eric Lacroix to stand.

'How do you plead Monsieur Lacroix?'

Mr. Dykes sprang up like a jack in a box. 'My client denies the charge,' and promptly sat down.

Fiona Black's heart sank. Bill Smith QC took the case in his stride. 'Then I call my first witness, Sergeant Rory Murdoch.'

Rory was called from the waiting room and made his way into the witness box. He looked around the court and pulled himself up straight to play his part in such an austere setting. He took the oath and turned towards Bill Smith QC.

'Sergeant Murdoch, how long have you been in the police force?'

'I've completed 29 years.'

Mr. Dykes got to his feet. 'Objection my Lord. Mr. Murdoch is based in Lamlash on the peaceful island of Arran. Somewhere I'd be happy to retire there. Twenty-eight years a policeman indeed. I doubt whether he has had to deal with anything more serious than a drunk driver. I wish to place on record that this officer's service is not tantamount to real police activity over the same period.' He then sat down and smiled at his aide, Des Delaney who had tipped him off to ask that question.

Lord McEwan responded. 'Mr. Dykes, I can't wait to hear you have retired to Arran but this interruption, and mark my words this has been an interruption, is irrelevant,' he said looking sternly at him. Then he nodded to Mr. Smith QC to continue.

'Thank you, My Lord. So how did you hear about the body in the field?'

'A holidaymaker, Mr. John Maxwell, reported finding the body decomposed in the field.'

'Objection. Where is this Mr. Maxwell as a witness?'

Mr. Smith replied instantaneously, depriving his Lordship any opportunity to make a ruling over the objection.

'The Crown did not feel Mr. Maxwell was significant in the chain of events and has not been cited accordingly,' said Mr. Smith staring at his adversary's colleague, Mr. Delaney.

'I am led to believe Mr. Maxwell did not find the body in the field at all, and that's why the defence wishes it to be recorded,' and then Mr. Dykes sat down.

'Mr. Murdoch, please tell the court who found the body initially,' asked Bill Smith, as Lord McEwan shook his head in despair over the procrastination on such a minor point.

'Mr. Maxwell's dog barked at something in the field. When Mr. Maxwell looked over the hedge, a bull was standing beside a withered skeletal hand. Mr. Maxwell phoned me at my office in Lamlash and that is how the case was notified. The press chose to refer to the finding having been made by the bull. That aside I went to see for myself and I found the decomposed body. Neither the dog nor the bull was cited to attend,' Rory added with a straight face. He saw Lord McEwan's generous smile.

'I think my friend can see why my colleague did not cite the bull,' Bill said looking at his opponent. He then turned his eyes to Rory once more.

'How old was the body?'

'It was thought to be over a year old and under two years. When a body is so far decomposed it is difficult to gauge the actual age.'

'Objection again, My Lord. Does Mr. Murdoch have a medical degree sufficient to conclude the body's decomposition rate? I mean it is crucial for my client. The body may have been in the field for a decade, I suggest. Unless Sergeant Murdoch has a medical degree......'

His Lordship's attention was fixed on Rory to respond.

'That was in the report which the forensic scientist, Dr. Jane Dunbar gave me. Here it is,' said Rory handing the forensic report to the clerk.'

Mr. Dykes QC lifted the report. He seemed to study it briefly then handed it over the desk to Mr. Smith, stretching out his hand then flicking it towards him.

'Exhibit No 1, My Lord,' said Mr. Smith QC.

'Very well. It is noted,' the learned Lord replied.

'Mr. Murdoch, how did the case proceed?'

'With great difficulty, I have to say. There was no clothing on the body, no known missing child on Arran as well as in Scotland, no known cause of death. The case died itself until a couple of months ago.'

'Then what happened?'

'I received a letter from the Governor of the prison at Charleroi. It told me of verbal communication between Mr. Lacroix and a fellow prisoner Guillaume Baratchart.'

'Objection. Is the court going to admit a verbal communication? Hearsay, I would call it.'

'It depends on what it is alleged Mr. Dykes. Shall we wait to find out?' Lord McEwan said as he grinned at Mr. Delaney. 'I shall reserve judgement at this stage.'

'And what was alleged to have been said Mr. Murdoch?'

'Mr. Lacroix revealed...'

'Can the sergeant please refer to my client as Monsieur instead of Mr?' Then Mr. Dykes sat down and crossed his arms.

'Carry on Mr. Murdoch,' said the judge.

Rory did not want to antagonise the Queen's Counsel any further. 'Monsieur Lacroix informed his cellmate that he had buried a body a couple of years ago on the Scottish Island of Arran. Additionally, that the body was of a relatively young Syrian girl in the process of being transferred by boat to Gourock where she was to be trafficked into sex and employed in a nail bar.' Rory raised the report from Guillaume Baratchart and the court official took it to show Mr. Dykes Q C who read it, then he once more floated the letter over the table to Mr. Smith QC.

'Exhibit number two, my lord. The letter is written in French. I wonder if my friend took enough time to translate it.'

'I assure you I have an 'A' in Higher French, Mr. Smith. I read French like cats drink milk.'

'You mean by that, you slowly lap up French?' teased Mr. Smith.

'Enough of this nonsense, gentlemen. Don't waste my time,' said his Lordship.

Then Mr. Dykes QC asked for a moment to speak to his client. Miss Black smiled at Rory. It seemed a significant moment on Mr. Dykes' part. The translator joined in the huddle.

'Mr. Dykes, in view of the apparent translation proceedings underway, I adjourn the case for fifteen minutes.' His Lordship's thoughts then returned to his chambers where his chin-dropping pipe was already filled with fresh St Bruno's tobacco and awaited to be lit.

He had no sooner mentioned the word adjournment than the court official rose to the occasion.

'Court rise,' he shouted as his Lordship left the bench.

Fifteen minutes later Rory returned to the witness box and was reminded he was still under oath. It was however unnecessary. Mr. Dykes stood up.

'My Lord, my client is now willing to accept the Syrian girl was murdered on board for refusing to engage in a sexual act with the crew members and she vowed not to work in a nail parlour. The traffickers did not wish the body to be found at sea and so a burial was agreed. As the boat approached Blackwaterfoot, a field was seen outside a cottage. It was dusk. There appeared to be no light and nobody in the cottage, so they dug a grave near a hedge out of sight of the occupants and buried the girl. My client accepts he murdered her and gives this explanation.' Thereafter he sat down.

Mr. Bill Smith QC stood up and his Lordship's eyes focussed on his. He was not expected to speak at this crucial point in the legal proceedings. The case for the Crown had been made and an acceptance of guilt recorded.

'My Lord, should the parents of the victim be found, an explanation of what happened to their daughter could be made if we knew her name.'

His Lordship looked at Mr. Dykes, who in turn looked at his client. He scribbled down a name.

'She was Jamal Badawi,' he informed the court.

# 19

The Court's ruling was a sentence of life in prison with a minimum of 32 years to be run concurrently with his Belgian sentence for trafficking. Eric Lacroix was taken to Kilmarnock prison to serve his life sentence shortly afterwards. There he must have reflected on his moment of madness in sharing his crime with his cellmate Guillaume, in Charleroi prison. Gone were the famous Belgian gourmet prison meals too. Porridge, potatoes, and white bread were to become his new prison diet.

Outside the court, the press collared Sergeant Murdoch and the next day, the whole of Scotland had read about the Belgian murdering trafficker in their papers. It was seen as a warning should any Scot dare to engage in this despicable trade, let alone murder.

On Jura, Constable Sammy Grant twiddled his thumbs in boredom at his desk after he had read the report of Eric Lacroix's case in his newspaper. He looked at the office clock. It was time to sneak out and cast his line.

Rory returned to his beloved Arran partly satisfied. He had achieved his conviction but there was one other murderer loose and the net just had to be closing in on Jim Randall, unless he had managed to reach the mainland and that would complicate the case. He had to assume Randall was still on the island.

Ella was pleased to see her father content and after a quick kiss, he retired to the kitchen to prepare a meal. They sat down in front of the BBC news and chatted between items. Hazel had spent the recent days taking Ella out in her mobile chair and she enjoyed the sun's rays on her face. On the seafront, she had had an ice-cream.

'Oh dear, an ice-cream,' Rory said looking down with an exaggerated look of disappointment.

'Why?'

'Because that's tonight's second course.' They laughed heartily.

'I don't mind,' said a smiling Ella.

The BBC Scotland news finished and then they saw in a weather forecast, an approaching front which appeared to be racing in from the west. It would land on Arran the next day said Kawser Quame the female weather forecaster. It would be depressing weather and Rory gathered the dishes and went back to the kitchen to prepare a fruit salad with ice-cream. Ella changed channels on her TV fob.

Suddenly Ella screamed. 'Dad you are on TV.'

Rory appeared at the open lounge door and saw the interview he had given on the steps of Ayr Sheriff Court.

'You should have your own programme on TV, Dad.'

Rory approached his daughter in her chair and tousled her hair. 'What do you mean a TV programme. Don't you mean I could be a Hollywood actor?'

Ella struggled to look backwards in her restricting chair but she managed to see her father. 'Yes, a film star. I'd like that.'

Two days later was a different day. The sun was up as early as Rory, the rooks were in chorus on different rooftops, the lawn had been cut late the night before as the rain had stopped mid-afternoon and the grass was almost dry.

Rory had taken one day's annual leave and he suggested they took the converted van around the island. Ella's eyes lit up. Rory made cheese and tomato sandwiches and washed a couple of apples. He took out two Tunnock's Caramel Wafers from the biscuit tin and filled one flask with tea and another with orange juice. They were ready for their day out.

Rory's sun visor remained down as the car ventured around the twisty southern part of the island. A splattering of white sheep decorated many fields and a big bird flew in front of the van.

'Did you see that?'

'Yes, what was it?' asked Ella straining to see its flight again.

'A goshawk,'

They stopped in a lay-by near Lagg.

'Too early for lunch?' Rory suggested.

'I agree, Dad.'

'I used to cycle down here when I was a schoolboy. From Lagg you could see the ships head down the Firth of Clyde. Sometimes American submarines too. Nuclear submarines, usually.'

'Did you ever want to work on a cargo boat or trawler?'

'No, but what I did do well was art. I used to draw coastal scenes always with a boat in the picture. Some were in the distance, but fishing trawlers had beautiful lines and I knew the details of them. I was first in Art class, year after year,' he said with a distant look of satisfaction recalling his happy schooldays. 'Okay, lunch in twenty minutes?'

Twenty minutes later they approached Blackwaterfoot. Rory drove down to the hotel and parked in its car park at the very front with a view across the sea to land somewhere between Campbeltown and Carradale.

As the sun's rays pierced the windscreen, they ate their lunch. The van was very warm. Rory lowered the window and a slight breeze entered. It was a soporific atmosphere and Ella noticed her father's eyes close. She did the same.

The rest did them both good. Their anxieties of the past few weeks abated there and then, and with his promotion and a successful operation behind her, Rory felt the world could not have provided a better day.

Just as they were setting off, Ella had a thought.

'You remember you said you found a hermit in the King's cave?' she asked.

Rory laughed. 'He was not a hermit. He was a retired policeman. What about him?'

'Well, the man you are looking for, Mr. Randall, I think he'd live around the coast where nobody would find him. He'd pass the King's cave at some point.'

Rory could not fault her reasoning. 'I guess so. He'd even have a reason to be around Blackwaterfoot.'

'Why?' Ella asked in puzzlement.

'His daughter, she was found on the sand, washed up on the shore not far from the hotel. Some murderers like to re-visit the scene of their crime. Perhaps it is how they try to come to terms with their guilt.'

As they passed the upper car park leading to the cave, Rory slowed down. Perhaps he might see Randall. But the car was soon passing the Machrie golf course and heading north, up the west coast.

At 3 pm they approached Lochranza. Rory decided to drop by and see Colin Nelson and parked in the police car park accordingly. He approached the desk as Nelson was coming out of his room. 'Ah Sergeant Murdoch,' he exclaimed. 'A social or business visit? Any news to report, you TV star!'

'Very funny Nelson. It's back to the day job now. But today is very much a social visit. I've Ella in the back of the car.'

'Oh, yup I guess you've earned a day off and you chose a fine day. Hey, wait a minute,' he said all of a sudden and disappeared into his room.

He returned with his hands behind his back. 'Let's go and see Ella,' he said.

They came back to the van and Nelson presented Ella with a box of Quality Street sweets. Her face lit up.

'That's very kind of you, Nelson.'

'Well, not really. It was a present from a local who appreciated what we were doing and of course, as you know, we are not allowed to accept gifts from the public.'

Rory smiled. This box was not destined to be going to the local care home. He knew it rounded Ella's day off with a welcome surprise.

# 20

Ella's comment played on Rory's mind. He had forgotten about Ron Glover. It was time to visit him again to see if Randall had been along that strip of coastline.

He arrived at the office to inform Lorna about his plan for the day.

'But not before your morning coffee, I am sure.'

Rory winked at Lorna. She knew him better than anyone. When the coffee arrived, the telephone rang.

'Hello, Sergeant Murdoch here. How can I help you?'

'D.I. Alan Barr here. I was feeling it was time to set foot in your patch. Just to get a feel for the island.'

'Of course, when would you like to visit, sir?' Rory asked finding his diary and biting off his pen top.

'No need for the formal. Call me Alan. There's no time like the present, today?'

There was a pause as Rory re-planned his day in his mind and assessed the forward-thinking D.I...

'Okay, today. Then the noon sailing from Ardrossan?'

'Just what I had planned.'

'I'll meet you at 1:06 pm.'

'1:06 pm it is. I'm looking forward to landing on Arran.'

'First time on Arran then, Alan?'

'Yes, shameful isn't it?'

Alan heard Rory laugh, so did he. Rory replaced the phone but kept his hand on the receiver for a couple of seconds. The new D.I. just had to be a better superior officer.

'Typical. I make a plan and it's a non-starter.'

Lorna grinned. 'Well, I'd like to meet the new D.I. anyway.'

'Yes, I'd like to show him around. I think he's a city boy.'

'Then I'll bring you the paper, the crossword is waiting.'

'Now that's a good idea.'

At 1:00 pm Rory was at the Brodick terminal. Local cars sped off the boat and some tooted Rory. Then the passengers made their way along the ramp into the terminal building. Rory stood outside the door. He had never met D.I. Alan Barr. A suited man approached and gave a broad smile. Rory looked around. It must have been for him. Then an arm was extended.

'Rory, good to meet you,' Alan said.

'Yes sir, I was looking forward to your arrival on God's island.

By the time they reached Lamlash, the D.I. had been appraised about Jim Randall, but not before congratulating Rory on the successful conclusion of the skeleton murder. There was even time for Rory to question the new boss about his past.

'I was a deputy director of Dolphin Brewin, an investment company. Got bored with finance eventually. Decided I wanted to contribute to society, so I joined the police on their graduate programme. I haven't got as much street credibility as you have, Rory,' he said smiling at him.

'But perhaps your street work was in Glasgow.'

'Pollok. Two and a half years there, three as a sergeant in Govan and now D.I. Ayrshire.'

'Rapid promotion,' suggested Rory.

'Yes, I suppose so but I'm a people's man, not a target-driven accountant policeman.'

'I'm glad to hear it. I'm sure you will get along well with Lorna.'

'Lorna?'

'She is my secretary. She is looking forward to meeting you.'


The afternoon flew by. Alan made a few suggestions like alternating white-capped road traffic policing one week and community policing the next which Rory agreed with and would adapt to his work. Catching the 4 pm ferry crossing sped them on their way back to Brodick. The D.I.'s visit had gone well.

On his return to Lamlash, Rory called in for his last half hour with Lorna.

'Well, what did you think of the new D.I.?'

'Think? He's drop-dead gorgeous. I'm sure you will get on with him.'

Rory smiled. What a relief, he thought. Such a pleasant change.

'Just a moment, Rory. There's one letter for you. I've read it and left it on your desk. I think it can't wait till tomorrow morning. You should really read it now,' she suggested with a wink that Rory could not really miss or understand.

In fact, Rory was puzzled. He sat down at his desk and then his blood ran cold. It was from the police station at Craighouse, the main town on Jura. He knew who had written it instantaneously. His hands were shaking as he lifted the single page to his eyes.

*Dear Rory*

*I trust you are keeping well. I hope your daughter is keeping well too.*

*I am writing to congratulate you on the successful conviction of that Belgian man. You did a fine job.*

*I have undergone my anger management classes and found them very useful. As you might have suspected one challenge I was given was to think of someone I don't like and write to him or her. Well, yes that is the assignment but what I am about to say is not part of that task.*

*I sincerely apologise for my attitude towards you. It was unprofessional and if I had appreciated more, the demands you had at home, I should have been more supportive. Yet I am not bitter that I am on Jura. I love the fishing here and have climbed one Pap already.*

*Finally, I wish you Rory, much happiness in your work and home life.*

*With sincere greetings*

*Sammy*

'Lorna, have you read what he said? Lorna...Lorna?' Rory looked at the office clock. Lorna had gone home. Rory took the letter and filed it in a folder marked Thankful Letters. Sammy's letter was now with a host of local letters of appreciation. As he closed the filing cabinet he smiled and shook his head. Sammy's letter had earned its resting place.

The following day had already been planned. Rory took the cross-island ribbon B road over to Blackwaterfoot. He parked in the village and set off by the beach. Soon the sand was behind him as he strolled along turf-pocked grass with seawater pools and clumps of pink thrift. Then boulders had to be mounted or circumvented and he felt his chest heaving. He lost his footing once or twice, but his ankles were encased in his standard-issued police boots. Soon he saw the cave in the distance but could see no human activity. He had come so far, there was no point returning at this stage. Eventually, as he approached, he shouted 'Ron' twice and a shadow appeared. He waved at Rory. They soon met and shook hands.

'I see you're a sergeant now,' said Ron admiring the stripes on each arm.

'Yes, came all of a sudden.'

'You must have deserved it; remember I know how the police work.'

Rory nodded. 'Yes of course. In fact, you might guess why I am here to see you?'

'No, not really. I've done with the police. You won't get me re-instated. I surface every now and then to restock, visit the bank but as you know, I spend a lot of time down here in all weathers. You can't imagine how therapeutic it can be.'

'You might not think so, but I understand, Ron. Some things just have to be done.'

Ron nodded and smiled. He knew Rory understood his grief.

'I was wondering if you had any visitors here, apart from me, that is?'

Ron looked up to the sky and watched a fluffy cloud fast approach the sun.

'When I hear visitors approach, I move out along the coast to the north. I let them see the cave and when they have gone, I return. It gets busy at times in the summer. For the rest of the year, I've usually got the place to myself.'

Rory took off his police cap and brushed the sweat from his brow with his arm. 'No individual visitors then.'

'No, I can't recall, well... there was one. A guy called Tony.'

'Tony?' Rory repeated.

'Yes, Tony...Tony Conway, he told me.'

'What was he like?'

'A bit like me, divorced,' he said. 'Coming to terms with it made him walk around the shoreline.'

'Local, was he?'

'Yes, I think so, quite local. Big man he was, didn't speak much.'

Rory shuddered. Big man fitted the bill. He tried to picture the man in his head. 'Did he say where he came from?'

'No, he didn't. But I think he was from Lochranza.'

'Lochranza, what makes you think that?'

'Well, he reminds me of a man I met in Lochranza, he was a clam fisherman.'

'You actually met him there?'

'No, I'm misleading you. I never met him. I watched him drag his boat from the sea one late afternoon and he had a net full of clams. He really looked like him. Poor man, divorced.'

'Which way did he go,' asked Rory almost swallowing his words in its rapid delivery.

Ron pointed north. 'He always comes from that way. I guess he's found his lonely spot too. It can't be far from here.'

Rory slapped Ron's shoulder. 'Don't be surprised if you see this place crawling with police. He's a wanted man. Wanted for murder. If he comes back don't give him cause to think you know about him. I'll be onto this right away.'

Ron's mouth opened in disbelief. Yet he was ex-police. He knew the importance of keeping silent in such matters. His eyes and ears would be used in support of his former police colleagues. He knew what it was like to be in the centre of a murder enquiry.

# 21

Rory lost no time contacting D.I. Barr. The message out was that Jim Randall was also known as Tony Conway and he was living between the King's Cave and Pirnmill. To be on the safe side Rory asked for six men to proceed south from Pirnmill and six to proceed north from Torbeg at the same time. Such a pincer-movement would flush him out. There was nothing to suggest Randall was armed but this ex-marine could be expected to put up a fight.

'Thanks, Rory, I can't give you all these men, sorry. I can spare four coming from Pirnmill and three from Torbeg. That should be enough. Seven men and a dog, a Vizsla. A police van will be on the road to collect him when he's arrested,' said the D.I. rubbing his hands and thankful Rory was now one of his diligent officers.

'But not an Alsatian, a Vizsla. Why?' Rory enquired.

'Hungarian Vizsla yes, Rubik by name. They are obedient, willing, and fast learners, good at pace over rough terrain. That's what you need here.'

'But can it show its teeth, can it detain a suspect till we arrive?'

'It's his pace is the thing. Rubik won't bite but he'll guard him so Randall won't move.'

'Okay, I'll take your word. It's a change from those sharp-toothed Alsatians.'

'Trust me, I know my dogs.'

The plan was an early start the following morning. Seven policemen in casual clothing but sturdy boots came off the early sailing of the day. The dog handler made sure his canine assistant, Rubik, found some grass before proceeding.

Within forty minutes both parties were in position and Rory instructed them to proceed. Both teams reported making progress with no sightings. Rory asked them to make sure every possible position was investigated.

The Pirnmill team was soon down at Machrie where the ground was flat. Then they followed the coastline as rocky stones slowed their progress.

The Torbeg team were making slower progress but were well on their way to the King's cave.

Then the Pirnmill team stopped. A freshly dug hideout appeared. It was a sizeable cavity in an earth bank. They approached it slowly and as silently as possible. But the stones were loose, and their footsteps were heard. Suddenly a man crawled out of the dugout and began to run away from the Pirnmill team. They shouted at him to stop. He didn't. They telephoned the Torbeg team to tell them that Randall was heading towards them.

They stopped and looked up. Their leader gave a signal for them all to drop to the ground. There was no exit for Randall. He would have to pass the Torbeg team so they spread themselves ten feet apart and settled down to await his arrival. They contacted the Pirnmill team to say they were in position and asked for all radios to be turned off.

The Torbeg team could hear the hurried steps of Randall as the stones were disturbed. They knew Randall was about sixty yards away. Then the dog handler set the Vizsla free and Rubik knew what he had to do. It headed straight for Randall. The police officers stood up to be seen and Randall realised the game was up. He raised his hands.

The Vizsla loudly barked three feet away from Randall.

'Get that dog away from me,' he shouted without taking his eyes off the barking dog.

'Rubik leave,' shouted his second-generation Hungarian handler, and the dog instantly sat down two feet from Randall and stopped barking. Its eyes fixed upon his. Randall's hands were still held in the air. The arrest followed immediately, and Randall was easily handcuffed and driven to Lamlash police station. Rory made friends with Rubik and appreciated the canine wisdom of Alan in selecting a Vizsla.

It was a pleasantly warm evening as Rory set off home. A good day's work was done, and he was well on the way to resolving Arran's three murders. Satisfaction was etched on his face and he marvelled at Ella's insight which had led to Randall's arrest.

Rory stopped off at the Lagg village store and bought the ingredients for the evening meal. He added a bottle of red wine once more. Celebration did not come often in his work, but no new murders had occurred and no outstanding cases gave him satisfaction which merited his glass of wine that night. Ella could have a small glass too but he felt it could well be an empty bottle when he went to bed that night.

He was surprised to see Maggie Ritchie's car still at the house when he arrived home. She usually had gone home by this time. As he got out of his police car another car drew up, alongside his. It was Dr. Black's.

They entered the house together as Dr. Black informed Rory that Nurse Ritchie had asked him round as Ella was in pain. Suddenly Rory went into shock. At least the appropriate medical staff were on hand. He needed to keep out of their way yet be told of every possible diagnosis.

Food poisoning perhaps, indigestion? Rory fought to think of any other explanation as Dr. Black prodded Ella's stomach just above her umbilical. He fixed his stethoscope to the same place. Ella's face was white with shock but Rory stood back to let the professionals decide what was wrong. He tried to catch Ella's eye to show her that her father was there, but her eyes seemed glazed and unfocussed.

Dr. Black looked at her eyes then again at her stomach. He placed his hand over her and pressed down. She groaned in pain.

'Mr. Murdoch, your telephone please.'

Rory took the telephone from the side table making sure the extended cable was not disconnected.

Dr. Black dialled. Rory saw him dial 999.

'Air Ambulance, Lamlash, female patient 17 years old. Renal failure with complications. You've got to avoid the Arran Clearance stones between the enclosures on Hamilton Terrace, just a reminder. The ambulance is what to look out for.'

He redialled. Rory failed to recognise the call.

'Ambulance to Murdoch, Willow Lane, Lamlash. Got it? Good. To helicopter pad at the front lawns.'

Dr. Black gave a long sigh. 'We've got to get Ella to the hospital quickly. You can travel with her. Perhaps you should pack an overnight bag. You'll need it.'

'You said renal failure with complications, doctor?' asked Rory.

'Yes, the complications are the spina bifida. But we must get her to hospital before it becomes acute.'

Rory understood the many ailments Ella had related to her condition. Always she recovered. She was a Murdoch and that meant she had guts, she was a fighter. Of that, he had no doubt.

The ambulance arrived at the helipad and Rory sat in it holding Ella's hand. He squeezed it and she squeezed his hand back. They seemed to reassure each other.

They kept warm in the ambulance. Some locals passed by and made their enquiries. The word would soon be out. Then a purr grew louder and the

Euro-copter EC 145 twin-engine helicopter landed in its red and white livery.

Medics from the helicopter first consulted Dr. Black then they moved Ella from the ambulance and slid her into position inside the helicopter. Rory told them he was her father and they directed him to a seat by his daughter and secured seat belts over him. In no time at all the craft was lifting in an initial angle towards the mainland, it left Arran.

It took twenty-five minutes to land on the Glasgow Western hospital roof where a nurse and a doctor were ready to receive Ella. Rory followed on breaking into pace to keep up with them. They entered a lift and it sped them down to the fourth floor.

The trolley made its way to the operating theatre and Rory was led into a waiting room. He sat down and tried to relax. He knew Ella was in the best place but he felt quite helpless.

A tea urn percolated noisily on a side table to his annoyance until he brought a paper cup to it and sampled the tea. It was what he needed. It calmed his nerves, slightly. The clock in the waiting room had already shown an hour had elapsed with no news. He hoped to collar a nurse to get some feedback but they all seemed busy flashing-by, near the door. None entered.

However, twenty minutes later a nurse entered the waiting room. She looked around then her eyes settled on Rory.

'Mr. Murdoch?'

Rory stood up instantly. 'Yes.'

'Come with me Mr. Murdoch, this way please.'

Rory concluded Ella was now in recovery and he would be able to comfort her. But he was walking away from the theatre.

'Please wait in this room,' the nurse said. 'Dr. Mohammad Abbasi will be with you in a moment.'

Rory was aware of the smallness of the room with the frilled curtains and a box of paper handkerchiefs on the side table. It was an ominous setting. Adrenalin flowed through his veins. He did not have long to wait.

Dr. Abbasi was a man of fifty years or so with greying hair. He extended his hand. They shook each other's hand.

'Please be seated, Mr. Murdoch. Ella has had spina bifida all her life and it has restricted much of her movement as you know. Sadly, we found she had acute renal sepsis and I am very sorry to tell you, that she did not recover from surgery. She did not suffer I assure you. She died at 19:18 this evening.'

A lump formed in Rory's throat. He always knew Ella was weak but the day he dreaded had arrived. With tears in his eyes, he looked up at Dr. Abbasi. 'Can I see her?' he pleaded.

'Of course, you can. I'll ask a nurse to accompany you. She will be with you shortly.'

Left alone in the room the sobs joined the tears Rory shed. He bit his bottom lip. He took a couple of tissues and tried to dry his eyes but they continued to produce tears. He suddenly felt very alone. No wife, no daughter. He did not want to return home to see his daughter's bedroom with all her possessions. It would be hard to do so. The nurse arrived.

'Are you ready, Mr. Murdoch?'

Rory's voice was lost. He simply nodded.

The nurse took hold of his arm. 'You will find Ella at rest looking asleep. You can touch her of course. Many like to stroke the deceased's hair or cheek. You may want to do that.'

But the word 'deceased' hit his throat hard. He entered the operation theatre where he found Ella. It was as if she was fast asleep. Her hair had been combed before he saw her. She looked content and lovely. He touched her cheek as he had done so often in the past. Each time she would turn and smile at him but now there was no response. Her left arm lay outside the sheets so he held her hand looking at her face but again no response. The truth dawned on him that his daughter was no longer there. Her body had freed her from all the pain she had endured throughout her life. That thought consoled Rory a tiny fraction. He took one last lingering look at his daughter then turned and left the theatre. There was much to attend to but first, he went into the waiting room once more and texted Lorna, the D.I., and Nelson.

The nurse followed him a moment or two later.

'We will be taking Ella to the mortuary. You are from Arran, aren't you?'

'Yes, Lamlash.'

'Then you will know who the undertakers are. They will collect her and take her back to Arran prior to burial or cremation. They will also bring her clothing and any personal effects she had, to your home.'

'I see,' was all Rory could say and in truth, he did not catch all she told him.

His mobile phone vibrated in his pocket. He retrieved it. It was a reply from Alan, the D.I. 'I'm dreadfully sorry to hear your sad news. Take two weeks off work immediately with full pay.'

# 22

Rory was amazed to find so many cards of condolences arrive on his carpet. They came from the Spina Bifida Society as well as some of Ella's fellow sufferers. The rest were from family and from every second house in town it seemed. Sad news travelled very fast but nothing compared to the speed of Lamlash.

It was while he was sorting the cards out and deciding which ones required a reply, the front doorbell rang.

When he opened it, he saw Wendy the French teacher, and his near neighbour. She carried a flask.

'It's vegetable soup. I always make too much,' she apologised.

'Come in, please do.'

'Thank you. Let me put the flask down here,' she said leaving it on the hall table. She entered the lounge.

Her eyes lit on the cards around the fireplace. 'Gosh, it shows how popular Ella was.'

'Yes, she had many friends.' However, Rory could not remember who they were, at that precise moment.

'But you were her best friend, not so?' Wendy asked.

Rory crossed his legs. 'Yes, after her mother died it was full steam ahead for me as bottle washer, cook, confidant and father to Ella.'

'I know. I've seen how devoted you were to her.'

There was a moment of calmness in silence and it was comforting for Rory.

'Can I ask what arrangements you have made for Ella?'

'Yes, she's at the Hendry Funeral services and that's where we will have the funeral service and then to the Masonhill Crematorium in Ayr.'

'I'll attend both,' she said

'That's not necessary. You have classes to take and it's a long way to Ayr and back.'

'Rory, I'm your neighbour and I want to help you as much as I can at this time.' Then she stood up to leave.

'I appreciate you calling to support me, Wendy. Oh, and the soup too. That's very thoughtful. Thank you again.'

Rory made an appointment with Dr. Black. He wanted to give his own tribute to Ella but did not feel confident he could do it without breaking down. Lexapro was prescribed and he started to take the course of tablets two days before the funeral.

The day was overcast. Gloomy one might say, and that was the state of most of the mourners which filled the funeral parlour. Surprisingly, a guard of four police officers in white gloves stood on the steps while neighbours, friends, and a few relatives entered sedately. He recognised D.I. Alan Barr and Nelson in the police guard. Ella's coffin was displayed at the front. Rory sat in the front row with his sister, Joan. Wendy was two rows behind as a neighbour and friend.

They sang one of Ella's favourite hymns, *Dear Lord* and *Father of Mankind*. Rory sang the bass line but in the penultimate verse his voice stuttered and hardness hit his throat. He had to remain silent till the moment passed.

> *Drop Thy still dews of quietness,*
> *Till all our strivings cease*
> *Take from our souls the strains and stress*
> *And let our ordered lives confess*
> *The beauty of thy peace*
> *The beauty of thy peace.*

After the hymn, Rory placed his order sheet on his chair and mounted the rostrum. He looked at the gathering. His eyes darted around so many familiar faces. As they took their seats, he cleared his voice.

> "How could I not grieve for you
> Your beauty and your smile
> How could I not grieve for you
> As I see you at this aisle.
>
> How could I not send love to you
> Despite our parting here
> You will always be with me
> Of that you need not fear.
>
> My life was blessed when you were born
> Despite the trials you bore

> Sometimes I could not sleep at night
> When hearing your long snore."

There was a hushed laugh at his last line. Rory looked up distracted but saw the smiling faces. They seemed to be enjoying and respecting his poem but also they were silently supporting him.

> "And so we part, our lives are severed
> But memories will remain
> Enhanced by your loving smile
> Cherished in wind, in sun and rain.
>
> Ella, sleep my precious until we meet again."

As Rory descended the rostrum, he heard sobs in the church and saw tears being wiped. Smiles of appreciation relaxed him. The funeral concluded with the funeral director inviting everyone to retire to the Douglas Hotel in Brodick.

Rory was glad to be in the company of his sister Joan and her husband Ian, who had come from their home in Kirriemuir. She had known Ella all her life despite the distance through postcards and letters which Ella enjoyed so much. Skype had more recently brought them together. It was because she had come to Arran that the cremation would be held two days later and Joan and Ian agreed to stay on for that.

'Thank goodness you will be at the Crematorium. There will hardly be anyone there. That's why we've had this service here today, Joan.'

'That was brave of you to give that poem. Did you...er ...did you write it?'

'Did it show?'

'No, I thought it very appropriate. Well done.'

Rory took a plate of sandwiches and mingled with the well-wishers. He offered Wendy his plate. She took a salmon and cress sandwich in brown bread.

'Thank you, Rory. Is that your sister you were talking to?'

'Yes, Joan and Ian. We don't really look alike, do we?'

'Not really,' they laughed. 'Must have a word with her,' she said and tapped Rory's wrist as she left. He smiled to see her approach his sister.

Rory continued to circulate. D.I. Barr stepped into his way.

'Rory, what can I say? You are a credit to the force. I did not realise how much work you would have had at home.'

Rory smiled at him feeling there might be a hidden message in what he said. Perhaps, I should now devote 100% to the force may have been what he was thinking? Then he thought better of the D.I. After all, he had no axe to wield at this Inspector.

'Thank you, Alan. Yes, I had two lives to lead but I enjoyed every moment. Ella was a wonderful daughter.'

'I am sure she was. I am sorry I never met her.'

'Have you heard how we trapped Randall?'

The D.I.'s eyebrows gathered together and his head tilted at the sudden change of subject. 'What do you mean Rory? I only arranged the men and Rubik. You were in charge. And you told me he was arrested.'

Rory smiled. 'Yes, that's true but how did I know to go to the King's cave?'

Alan remained perplexed for a moment. Then it became clear to him. 'Ah, I see. Local knowledge?' he suggested.

'In a way, yes. Ella told me to go there.'

The day before they set off for Ayr, a police van arrived at Rory's house. He watched as the car door opened and Rubik made straight for a lamppost.

'Hi Rory, can I come in?'

Rubik took the cue from his master. Then Flop met Rubik and they started to tease each other by tearing around the hall.

'Looks like they get on well together.'

'You know I'm not back at work till next week?' said Rory trying to identify the reason for his appearance.

'Sure, that's why I called. When you get to Ardrossan, before the crematorium at Ayr tomorrow, let me take Flop and we'll go for a walk. Better than having the dog in the house all day.'

'That's very good of you, Gergely. Come into the lounge. Let me brew you a tea or a coffee.'

'Tea for me, one sugar and milk please.'

Rory entered the kitchen and filled the kettle. He shouted through to the lounge.

'So Hungarian by birth, may I ask?'

'No, can't you hear my accent? As Ayrshire as you can find it,' his bass voice bellowed. 'My parents escaped the Hungarian Rising in 1956. Dad's brother was executed by the Russians. He was a demonstrating student. Mum and Dad were young and were among the 20,000 who escaped. Over 2,500 Hungarians were killed and 700 Russian soldiers.'

'Wow, that was tough going. So how did they end up in Ayrshire?'

'Mining was Dad's trade. Dalmellington was looking for miners and so he came here. Simple as that. That's where I was born, Gergely Losouczy. Primary 1 Dalmellington is where it all started,' he said with Flop sitting comfortably on his lap, much to Rubik's surprise.

'In fact, it was where I learned discipline. I used to get teased, you see. The kids at school nicknamed me Lucy. You can imagine how I reacted.'

'Fists?'

Yes, you got it right,' he laughed. 'I was sent before the headmaster twice for fighting but when he heard what I was being called; he soon put a stop to it. Did you have a school nickname?'

'Me, a nickname? No. I've always just been Rory.'

Flop jumped down from Gergely's lap and jumped up on Rory's. 'Are your parents still alive?'

'No, only my mother, she's still in Dalmellington and that's where I'll take the dogs tomorrow. I've a few days' leave to take off, anyway. Not back till the following week as a witness when Randall is on trial at the High court in Ayr.'

'I thought he might shorten his sentence with a plea bargain,' suggested Rory sipping his mug.

'Delaney tried to go for the lesser charge of manslaughter through diminished responsibility. Fiona Black would not have it. It's murder with a trial.'

'You said Delaney?'

'Aye, he's a hard nut to crack,' said Gergely rubbing Rubik's head as he did so.

Two days later they arrived at the Masonhill cemetery in Ayr. A retired cleric gave a somewhat impersonal address and then the curtains closed during his final prayer. Rory focussed on the disappearing coffin and despite a lump in his throat, he smiled. He was proud to have known and loved Ella, as his one and only daughter.

# 23

The postman rang the front doorbell. Rory threw his dishtowel over the un-dried plates and opened the door.

'Morning Rory, a parcel for you to sign.'

'Mmm Bill, I'm not expecting one. Sure it's for me?'

The postman turned the box over. 'It says Mr. Rory Murdoch with your address.'

Rory signed and noticed an Ayr postmark. He thanked Bill his regular postman and entered his lounge. Flop looked up then ignored the box as there was no food scent in it. Rory brought through a sharp kitchen knife and opened it. It was a box containing a letter. He opened the letter. It was from the Crematorium. He had Ella's ashes on his lap.

That night his doorbell rang again. Wendy appeared with a box.

'My goodness a second box today,' he found himself saying. 'Come in.'

Wendy placed the box on the sideboard.

'May I look inside?' asked an interested Rory.

'Please do.'

Rory eased the lid off and turned over the covering greaseproof paper. He helped himself to one.

'Those are Langues de Chat. Underneath is a layer of Tuiles aux Amandes. That is if you are not allergic to nuts,' she grinned.

'Hmmm good and I don't think they were made in France, they are still warm,' he mumbled as he digested a couple of Langues de Chat.

Wendy shook her head. 'It follows, doesn't it? I teach and bake French.'

Rory helped himself to the almond biscuit and then held the box in front of Wendy. She put her hand up to protest. 'They are for you, all of them.'

'My, I am getting spoiled by you.'

'Just some needed attention. The past few days must have been challenging. I felt you needed some TLC perhaps.'

They sat down with Flop sitting on her feet.

'Tell me. May I ask you?' Rory almost stuttered. 'Grief, how long does it last?' he asked.

'Ray had lung cancer. I knew he would die. I was prepared for it. That was almost four years ago and I don't mind admitting I often take moments to think about him. But they are not sad times. They have disappeared. I enjoyed our holiday times, Christmas meals, and all the fun times come back.'

Rory thought for a moment. 'Holiday times? I can't rely on them.'

'Why?'

'I've never been away for the last seventeen summers. I could not. It would have been too difficult for the two of us.'

Wendy hesitated for an instant then she plucked up courage. 'Did you know I still have a time-share in Nouvelle-Aquitaine? I kept it going even after Ray's death. You'd love it there. It's by the sea and it is very warm in summer. Guaranteed heat, I assure you.'

'I could dream of that certainly.'

'I'd prefer you to think about it seriously. I could do with the company and you could do with a holiday.'

'Put it that way, I could hardly refuse,' Rory smiled with a warm feeling deep inside he could hardly explain or deny.

Wendy bent down to stroke Flop. The dog responded by rolling over wishing its tummy rubbed. Wendy obliged. Then she looked up at Rory. 'Tomorrow, I will be cooking Gibelotte de Garenne. There will certainly be enough for two. Would you like to come over?'

'Gibel... de what? Are you going to poison me?' he laughed.

'It's good to hear you laugh, Rory. 'I'll not poison you, after all, we don't want a fourth Arran murder do we?' They both laughed this time.

'It's marinated rabbit casserole. I got a fresh rabbit from David McKinnon, the Arran Butcher.'

'Ah oui, then it's bound to be good,' said Rory proud to have uttered two words in French.

They talked for another two hours that Friday night about the murders, her teaching, and the occasional child known to them both reported to the police and then to the children's reporter or procurator fiscal. It was almost 11.15 pm when Wendy got up to go home. As she was leaving the front door, Rory was just behind her. A moment's silence ensued and then Wendy turned around.

They gingerly drew nearer and kissed each other good night. It may have been only a brief peck on the lips but for Rory, it was an earth-shattering moment.

The following night Rory arrived at Wendy's house with a bottle of wine, French of course, and a box of Black Magic chocolates. As he entered the house, he smelt the casserole and its aroma was very appetising. He was met with a brief kiss on his cheek this time and Rory realised the previous night's kiss was meant after all.

Wendy's house was the same size as Rory's but the colours in the lounge were softer. When Wendy made her request to Alexa, Rory did not hear what she said. He was familiar with the music playing but could not name it. He enquired.

From the kitchen, Wendy shouted through, 'Rachmaninov's Piano Concerto Number Two.'

'Ah, I knew it,' he said shaking his head in disappointment more than the disbelief of not identifying it sooner. 'Can I help you with anything?'

'No, thanks. The table is set, the wine is on the sideboard, the casserole needs a few more minutes and the vegetables are still a wee bit hard. Time for a sherry I think.'

She came back to the lounge. Wendy poured Rory a sherry and they clinked glasses.

'To us,' said Wendy.

Rory thought as he smiled back. He felt they were indeed becoming a partnership. 'Yes, to us,' he agreed. 'Tell me, why did you become a French teacher? Was it the Auld Alliance?'

'I suppose you could say that but I got off to a good start. My late mother, Alice Vuillermoz, was French. And I met Ray when we were doing modern languages at Glasgow University. He studied German.'

'Do you speak German too?'

'Yes, and some Spanish as well. Modern Studies we call it these days.'

'Then I'm out of your league.'

Wendy placed her glass on the mantelpiece. She sat down beside Rory on the sofa.

'Nonsense. Rory, you are a gentleman. A thoughtful and caring individual. One I am lucky to find. Yes, our occupations are so different but I sense compatibility between us.'

These were words that Rory was pleased to hear. He thought seriously about his future, new chapters were being written at a rapid rate. He had to let go of the past, he told himself. He felt young enough to set forth and he did so.

'Wendy, I'm... sure...I am in love,' he managed to stutter out.

'With me, I hope?' she replied in rapid fire.

'I assure you, I have no one else in mind.'

Suddenly the moment had gone. 'Good gracious, the vegetables.'

# 24

Having taken the early boat to Ardrossan, Rory was in Ayr sheriff court by 9:45 am. Fiona apprised him of developments. Randall had attended a first appearance at which Des Delaney had invited the court to seek a psychiatric report on his client. That report had been completed and Fiona had been given a copy. She told Rory that Jim Randall had been declared of sound mind and so fit to stand trial on murder and not the lesser *nomen juris* of manslaughter.

The jury was sworn in. Rory was the first witness. He gave the oath after his entrance to the witness-stand and the duration of his police service.

Gordon Carruthers QC arose from the same table where Fiona sat. 'Officer, give the court the events which led to Mr. Randall's arrest.'

'The child's body was quickly identified as Ruth Dynes. We went to her house in Lochranza to inform her parents. Only her mother was in. Her step-father Mr. Jim Randall was out in his boat, clam-fishing.'

'Did you bring Mr. Randall in for questioning?' Carruthers asked.'

'Not initially. He went into hiding after we discovered his partner's body in his house, the following morning.'

'Objection,' declared Nigel Bain QC on the prompting of Mr. Delaney. 'The officer has not linked Mr. Randall's disappearance and the murder of his wife. My client will tell the court he was on an extended clam fishing trip.'

'Mr. Bain, we will presumably hear such evidence from your client in the fullness of time,' said Lord Anderson, the trial Judge who then nodded to Mr. Carruthers to continue.

'As you were saying officer, you traced Mr. Randall to a cave, not so?'

'Yes, that is right. We had a tip-off and set a pincer movement with officers coming from both north and south. Mr. Randall appeared from his dugout. Then he was apprehended and charged with both murders.'

Mr. Carruthers QC sat down satisfied that he had got off to a good start.

Mr. Bain QC got to his feet, tugged at his gown around the collar, and looked straight into Rory's eyes.

'Let me get it clear. You went to the house to inform Ruth Dynes and her partner that their daughter's body had been found.'

'Yes, that is correct. Except Lizzie was the daughter of Ruth Dynes and step-daughter of Mr. Randall.'

'You learned that her step-father was out fishing but as it was late afternoon, you decided not to question him.'

'That was a mistake. Had we taken him into police custody that night, there would not have been a second family murder.'

'Supposition Mr. Murdoch, supposition. The fact remains you did not really suspect Mr. Randall, or you would have waited.'

Rory felt he had made his point and after all what he said was not a question.

Mr. Bain looked around the court then scanned the faces of the jury. 'I have no further questions.'

Mr. Carruthers then called forensic pathologist Dr. Jane Dunbar.

Rory was pleased to see Dr. Dunbar again. He felt she was bound to assist the case head further forward.

'Dr. Dunbar, what were your findings in Ruth Dynes' murder?' asked Mr. Carruthers QC.

'I examined Ruth both at the location on the shore where she was found and in the mortuary. At the beach, it was clear it was a case of murder. Her throat was heavily bruised. There was no doubt that strangulation caused her death approximately three or four days beforehand.'

'And can you explain how her body was washed ashore?'

'At the mortuary, there was extensive bruising on her right ankle. When thrown overboard somewhere between Lochranza and Blackwaterfoot she received this injury.'

'Objection. A bruise on the ankle cannot conclude her body was thrown overboard from a boat.'

'Dr. Dunbar, perhaps you can retract that statement,' his lordship requested.

'Your honour I did not fully explain. The injury was not just bruising. A skelf, a fragment of wood, was impaled in her ankle. It was consistent with the red paint as found on Mr. Randall's clam-fishing boat.'

There was a hush around the court. The Judge looked at his watch. 'I think this is an appropriate time to break for lunch. We will resume this case at 2 pm.'

'Court rise,' the court official shouted in decibels which shook the rafters.

Rory's evidence was over. He should have started his return journey to Arran but he hesitated on the seafront. What was he going back to when Ella's needs were no longer required to be met? He sauntered along the seafront taking in the sea air. He looked over to the silhouette of Arran's Sleeping Warrior Mountains. Then he watched as a long ribbon of waves gently tickled the golden sands of Ayr. After a few more reflective minutes he returned to the town and entered the Wellington Bar. He ordered a lasagne with garlic bread. He was eating plenty of European fodder he realised.

As the hour struck 2 pm, the court resumed but Mr. Bain was in deep discussion with Mr. Randall. Mr. Carruthers looked towards the bench but the judge just raised his pen to silence him. Then Mr. Bain QC stood up and faced the judge.

'M' Lord, my client now accepts he did kill his step-daughter and common-law wife, respectively Miss Lizzie Dynes and Mrs. Anne Dynes on the days stated in the charge, last April. I have nothing more to add,' he sat down with a glance across the table.

The Judge held the court in suspense as he scribbled some notes. Then he looked at Mr. Randall.

'Mr. Randall, please stand.'

Jim Randall looked less of a retired soldier and clam fisherman and more like a down and out. His head was bowed. The judge felt it inappropriate to have him stand straight. He would not prolong his agony.

'You have admitted the foul and despicable murders of your step-daughter and your common-law wife. Two women who, understandably, could not withstand your brute force. You have shown no remorse. I order you to serve life imprisonment with a recommendation of serving twenty-nine years.'

The judge looked up to the court official and that was his signal to shake the rafters once more.

'Court Rise.'

Mr. Carruthers QC shook Fiona Black's hand.

'Two murders on Arran. That takes some believing.'

'Two murders, don't you mean three?' she asked.

# 25

On his return home, Rory questioned his future. Wendy had appeared out of the blue yet he seemed ready to share his life with her. Was it too soon to move forward with the relationship?

On the ferry home, he took out his phone and called the Kirriemuir number.

'Hi, Joan, Rory here. How are you and Ian?'

'Fine and you?'

'On the ferry home after a successful outcome. Thought I'd share that news with you. I guess it will be in the papers tomorrow.'

'Sounds like that other murder you told me about,' she suggested.

'This was the double murder.'

'You are certainly hitting the papers these days.'

'Yes, all these Arran murders. I hope it does not put off visitors to the island. As you know tourism is their life-line.'

'It certainly is. On another point, err...Wendy... certainly seems keen on you,' said Joan.

'Hey, how did you know that?' asked Rory.

'I spoke to her at Ella's funeral. Remember?'

'Oh yes, of course.'

'Have you seen her since?'

The line was momentarily silent.

'What if I told you I intend to marry her?'

Joan laughed. 'Just what you need, another woman in your life. I don't think you could have found a nicer person.'

Rory smiled. 'Glad to have your opinion.'


Rory could not remember the drive from the ferry to Lamlash. He parked outside Wendy's house. It was 3.30 pm. He knew she'd return at 4 pm. He sat in the car with many thoughts filling his head. In his mind, he heard his wife and Ella urge him to go ahead. As the minutes passed by his anxiety increased. He checked his pocket. It was still there, gleaming as it had been in Warren James jewellery shop in Ayr where he had stopped to purchase it after court. Two cars had gone by since he parked his car. It was the third one that caused his heart to leap. Wendy's car drew up facing his own. She turned off the engine as Rory was getting out of his.

'Time for a cuppa?'

'Sounds good to me,' replied Rory as Wendy pecked him on the cheek. They mounted the steps leading to her house. She took her keys from her handbag and placed one in the door. The door opened. Wendy went in first and turned to let Rory in but he was not there. He had bent down on the final step and his hand was in his pocket.

Wendy's eyes enlarged. Her mouth hung open.

'Wendy, I love you. Would you be willing to make my life complete once more and be my wife? Will you marry me?'

Rory rose and opened the jewellery box. He took out the engagement ring and placed it on her finger. It fitted like the proverbial glove.

'Come here. They hugged as she whispered in his ear. 'Of course, I'll marry you. Of course, I will.'

The following Saturday on a gloriously warm sunny day, Rory and Wendy set off to the Holy Isle ferry. They parked on some flat land just above the slipway.

'David, you ready for us?' Rory asked the boatman.

'Aye, jist a moment.'

A few holidaymakers took a look at the sailing times. It seemed that the ferry was about to leave early. They rushed to the ferry hut.

'Can we get to the Holy Isle on this sailing?'

'Sorry, this is a private sailing but look at the board here,' he said pointing to it. 'We will be back soon and then I'll take you over. We won't be too long. Go and have an ice-cream or a coffee at the corner shop up there,' he pointed.

'Have we time for a cup of tea?'

'I won't go without you.'

Rory and Wendy stood on the quay and saw David come towards them.

'Are you all right Rory?' asked Wendy holding his arm.

Rory bit his lip, nodded his answer, and smiled at Wendy realising a tear might drop at any time.

They were assisted onto the boat and found a seat at the stern of the small ferry. On Rory's lap sat Ella's ashes, in a plain box.

'Why at the Holy Isle, may I ask, Rory?'

He looked at her rather sheepishly. 'Because it's the same journey I took seventeen years ago.'

Wendy gave a gently melancholic smile. She held Rory's hand and rested her head on his shoulder.

As they approached eight minutes into the journey, David cut the engine. They were approximately halfway between Whiting Bay and the Holy Isle. Silence came over the party as Rory stood on the port side of the vessel. Wendy stood beside him holding her hands around his waist to steady him.

Rory had brought a small trowel with him. He opened the box and saw once more the grey gritty ashes of his daughter. He dug the implement into the box then cast the first of the ashes into the water. Some dust flew back on his face and so they moved to the stern of the boat where the wind was behind them.

In silence, Rory thought not of Ella's many ailments but of her smile and the love she showed each day towards him. He was fulfilling the final act of the funeral, seeing the ashes float away in the very deep water beneath them. Ella was free to travel anywhere and everywhere and every time Rory's eyes settled on the sea, he knew Ella was there. He gave the box a final shake then waved a last farewell at the rippling waves. Then he sat down. He looked up at David and nodded to him. The engine started to grumble and they returned to Whiting Bay.

Two months later at the Brodick registrar's office, Wendy and Rory were married with Nelson as best man, and Joan and Ian were in attendance. They returned to Wendy's home where a large plate of Salade de Céleri Rémoulade had been prepared and after the celeriac with Rémoulade sauce, they had hot Crème Bachique followed by traditional wedding cake.

It was no surprise their honeymoon was in Paris where they spent a week sightseeing and eating well especially at La Mamie Bidoche on the rue de Candie in early June.

Six weeks later, during the summer school holidays, they spent three weeks at Wendy's timeshare at Lacanau Ocean in the Bay of Biscay. Rory practised skimboarding and swam. He ran along the beach and dived into the advancing waves.

In the pine woods behind the golden spotless sands, they threw large pinecones at each other frequently missing but if hit, a consoling cuddle was the loser's gain.

They visited nearby Bordeaux and had lunch at le Parc Marceau before walking around the city centre.

'Look there,' said Rory. 'That street!'

Wendy turned to see what interested him and saw immediately. Rue David Johnston.

'He came from Scotland to Bordeaux and in 1734 began a wine business. It's a very famous wine business and is still thriving today as Nathanial Johnston et Fils,' said a knowledgeable Wendy who knew the street well from previous years.

As they sauntered in the heat with only a feather-light breeze, a man suddenly shouted.

'Attention regarder un voleur de vélo.'

Wendy grabbed Rory's arm. 'He says that young lad on that bicycle is a thief.' She pointed at him as his cycle approached.

Rory shook Wendy's arm free. Instinct took hold of him. He pushed her against the building on the pavement. As the cyclist was about to speed by, Rory stepped into his way at the last moment and grabbed him around the chest. The boy's hands left the handlebars and he fell off his bike. Rory pounced on top of him.

The shouting had alerted two gendarmes and they came running towards Rory. So too was the man whose bike had been stolen. He carried a broken security chain in his clenched hand.

Wendy rushed forward to see if Rory was injured.

'Just a scrape,' he said as the police arrested the youth. An officer seemed to be speaking to Rory. 'What did the policeman say?'

'He says it was lucky the thief was not carrying a knife. They often do. You were very brave sir.'

'Tell him I knew what I was doing. I'm a Scottish policeman.'

'Il dit que c'était de l'instinct, il estun policier écossais.'

The gendarme smiled. 'Ah bon. Il fera un bon témoin.'

'What was that he said?'

'He said 'Ah good. You'll make a good witness.'

Rory's eyes lit up. He'd have to wait for a court date. And he did not speak French at all. He looked very serious. Yet the policeman smiled.

'Il n'y aura pas de tribunal. Il vient d'admettre sa culpabilité,' he said.

Wendy held Rory's arm, smiled, and patted it. 'It's all right Rory; the thief has just admitted his guilt.'

'Mais pour la formalité, nous aurons besoin du nom et de l'adresse de votre mari. S'il vous plaît.'

'Bien sûr,' said Wendy. 'Rory give me your business card.'

Rory opened his wallet with a wondering look. He handed his card over.

The policeman smiled as he placed it in his notebook. 'Je suis reconnaissant à vous monsieur pour votre aide dans son arrestation. Merci.'

Rory smiled as the policeman did and repeated a familiar word 'Merci'. Then le gendarme joined his colleague in his van and set off with the culprit seated in the back looking dejected.

Wendy shook her head and grinned. Rory looked at her. 'The very first occasion a stranger referred to you as my husband, was a Frenchman,' she said.

'Somehow I'm not surprised,' Rory replied. 'Let's get back to the beach. I'm really not a city man.'

'Great idea. And today, I'm going to be even more French.'

Rory did not understand. 'What do you mean?'

Wendy stood on her tiptoes and whispered in his ear.

'Topless, like the rest on the beach.'

Wendy encouraged Rory to learn and speak some French and soon he was purchasing the daily baguette. It was relaxing for them both although Rory would talk about this French holiday almost every week until they returned the following year. His holiday spirit had returned after many years.

On returning to his police desk at Lamlash, the phone rang.

'It's a Mrs. McWhirter for you, Rory,' shouted Lorna.

The name didn't mean much to him. He lifted the phone wondering what her concern would be. It could not possibly be another murder. It transpired that Mrs. McWhirter's Border terrier had slipped its lead and was missing.

'And what's the dog's name? .... Rover?' Rory smiled. Rover was true to form; he seemed to be a wild rover.

'I'll attend to it without delay,' he said.

He would have kept to his word but he had a pressing need. A mug of his ground Guatemalan coffee was only half drunk.

The End

La fin

# Interview With The Author

## Why was the setting primarily on Arran?

Arran is Scotland's third largest island. Yet it is compact. I have holidayed at Machrie and Blackwaterfoot and know all the towns, glens, sands and walks.

But when I befriended the black bull and thought I saw a skeleton, I had the first chapter planned. It was easy to imagine being anywhere on Arran because I have been everywhere on Arran.

## There were two High Court scenes. Did they create challenges in writing about them?

Before I retired to write books, I prosecuted in Sheriff Courts at Kilmarnock, Ayr and Dumfries. I knew the tricks some defence lawyers used. The High court has the same rules as the Sheriff courts but with Queen's Counsel lawyers so it was not difficult to set these murder trials in the High Court. They had to be on the mainland and that meant the High court would sit at the Ayr Sheriff Court. Many alleged offenders claim 'not guilty' but they often cave-in to get a lighter sentence when they realise the game is up. And yes, both court's officials really do shout 'Court Rise.'

## A novella, not a novel. Why?

I wanted this book to be a fast paced story without being too laden with words. I knew the plot in my head and three murders were both feasible and believable within a novella. Novellas are coming back into fashion. Bumper novels have had their day. But I admit this is the shortest story I have had published.

## The emotions are laid bare in the story. Were these chapters easy to write?

When writing about death and murders there are always survivors to think about and their grief. I don't deny a lump in my throat at such times when writing but when a child dies tears can fall from my eyes. If emotions are awakened in the reader, then the author has achieved the required effect.

## Why place the photos in the book?

I was looking through my Arran photographs and realised I had referred to many locations in the book. The bull did exist and gained two photos. That bull really did inspire the story. Text with the pictures reinforces the scenes being read.

Finally, isn't Arran a wonderful island and very photogenic too? I have no relationship with the Arran Tourist Board, but I'd be the first to recommend it as the most relaxing holiday island where there is so much to do.

## Which of your books stand out?

Both **A Reluctant Spy** and **Caught in a Cold War Trap** have been optioned by ARTE, a French Film company. Why French Films? Because my agent Mathilde Vuillermoz is French. That is the first stage. Perhaps next year might see how far they go to become films. *There's many a slip 'twixt the cup and lip.*

## Which is your favourite book you have written?

**The Parrot's Tale** is my favourite because it has a lot of comedy in it. It has a feel-good chuckle factor.

## What are you writing now?

It's too soon after writing this story, so I'll spend time with the Jane Austin Literary Foundation. Then suddenly, like the bull, another story will settle in my mind**.**

## Note:

Do you want to discuss this book or any other I have written? Use my e-mail to invite me to your book group. I charge nothing but appreciate a cup of tea and travel costs if appropriate. Contact me at **netherholm6@yahoo.com**

Since 2019 I have been working as a Jane Austin Literary mentor, supporting evolving children writers all over the world. A writing career offers many opportunities. I am delighted to be working with children from Saudi Arabia and Qatar so far. I will be reading what Ghanaian children have written soon.

# PHOTOS

*The real holiday home where the first chapter was written.*

*Here is the bull which inspired this story at the hedge where the skeleton was found.*

*John and Morag Maxwell's collie, Georgie, on holiday on Whiting Bay beach.*

*Blackwaterfoot, Arran. Yet another body to investigate.*

*Deer on the Lochranza golf course, in all weathers.*

*Lochranza – the home of the Randall family.*

*Entering King's Cave. Ron Glover's hideaway.*

*Four Police officers approached from this route heading north to capture Jim Randall near the King's cave.*

*This is Lamlash seafront with the Holy Isle in the background. Ella's resting place.*

*The boat to the Holy Isle, which took Ella's ashes.*

*Once more, the friendly bull I got to know and the instigator of this story.*

# OTHER BOOKS BY MILLER CALDWELL

## Novels

### *Operation Oboe*

A Scottish widow becomes a Second World War spy in West Africa

ISBN 0755200090-X New Generation Publishers

### *The Last Shepherd*

An arrogant city banker clashes with the rural ways of the last shepherd in south-west Scotland.

ISBN 978-07552-0643-4 New Generation Publishers

### *Restless Waves*

A writer-in-residence aboard a cruise ship faces daemons on board and onshore.

ISBN 0-7552-0260-0 New Generation Publishers

### Miss Martha Douglas

Martha, a nurse and seamstress, obtains a royal position but becomes a suffragist. When released from prison she serves in the trenches, where she finds true love.

ISBN    978-0-7552-0689-6    New    Generation Publishers

### The Parrot's Tale

The comic tale of an escaped parrot in the Scottish countryside sits alongside the tragedy of a missing girl.

ISBN 978-1-910256-05-3

 New Generation Publications


### Betrayed in the Nith

In this modern romantic novel set in south west Scotland, fraternal devotion turns to an unexpected romance as the mystery of Danny Kimber's death comes to light.

ISBN    978-07552-0625-4    New    Generation Publishing

## The Crazy Psychologist

Set on Rousay in the Orkney Islands, the childhood difficulties of Dr Angle Lawrence come to light, explaining her bizarre treatment programmes, while her fragmented family come to terms with their past, placing her marriage in jeopardy.

ISBN 978-1-910667-24-8 Matador Publishers

## The Trials of Sally Dunning and A Clerical Murder

(Two novellas in one book.)

### The Trials of Sally Dunning

Sally Dunning is autistic. Bullied, defrauded and drugged, she is not likely to be the best witness as she sees goodness in everyone. However, a chance meeting on holiday when her home is burgled turns Sally's life around in a spectacular way.

### A Clerical Murder

Dr Tony Scriven has a cross-section of clerics on his psychiatrists list. He notes they are all musical. Group therapy is part of his treatment for them. But what changes do the clerics experience? When a cleric is murdered it seems obvious who did it. But is it? Can the patients ever be the same after their encounter with the psychiatrist? And can love be found in the mayhem?

ISBN 978 1788038 126 Matador Publishers

## *A Lingering Crime*

Jack Watson is arrested and charged with murder. Extradition takes him to Florida but he has never been there before. Florida still has the death penalty and his thoughts turn to the electric chair. But did he know the victim? How could he be linked to the deceased? As Jack's story emerges, we learn of his troubled past and his need to right wrongs.

ISBN 978 1789014 150 Matador Publishers

## *A Reluctant Spy*

The life story of Hilda Campbell, who became Frau Hilda Büntner Richter before Lady Hilda Simpson. A double agent in World War 2.

ISBN 978-1-912850-64-8 Published by Clink Street.

## *Caught in a Cold War Trap*

Listening to a radio Moscow broadcast, Glasgow schoolboy Robert Harvie finds errors in the programme which he reports to the Russians. Then as a student Robert accepts a grant from the Russian Embassy and so he is inadvertently compromised. His first mission takes him to Ghana where murder is his first assignment. How can he escape?

Clink Street publishers

ISBN 978-1-913136-78-9

## <u>Biographies</u>

### *Untied Laces*

The author's autobiography. He confronted Osama bin Laden in Abbottabad, brought an African dictator to tears, and has two international sporting caps. So why did untied laces trip him up?

ISBN 978-07552-0459-5

New Generation Publications

### *Jim's Retiring Collection*

The illustrated cartoons and musings of a city and then rural Church of Scotland minister. Gathered and set in biblical context.

New Generation publications

ISBN ASIN B00ND 3F7PM

*Poet's Progeny*

A line of descent of the national bard, Robert Burns, maintains his influence over succeeding generations.

ISBN 0-7552-0178-7

New Generation Publishing

*7 point 7 on the Richter Scale*

The diary of the camp manager in the NWFP of the Islamic Republic of Pakistan following the 2005 earthquake. (Profits have gone to Muslim Hands for earthquake relief)

ISBN 978-0955-47370-8

Alba Publishers

## Take the Lead

The quirks of dogs, as experienced by the author over his life in Scotland, Pakistan and Ghana, together with canine poetry with a record of medical advances made by our canine friends understanding human conditions.

ISBN 9-781910256213

Netherholm Publications

## CHILDREN'S BOOKS

### Chaz the Friendly Crocodile

Chaz the Nigerian crocodile visits a Scottish river to help people keep their towns tidy. Set as a poem, this is a book parents can use to teach their growing children the value of good manners.

ISBN 978-1-84963770-1

Austin Macauley

### Lawrence the Lion Seeks Work

There are no more animals in the circus. So what happened when Lawrence the lion went in search of a new job?

ISBN 978-0-75521656-7 Netherholm Publications

### *Danny the Spotless Dalmatian*

Dalmatian puppies have no spots at birth; they appear after three weeks. But Danny's spots never appeared. Follow him as he searches for spots to make him a real Dalmatian.

ISBN 978-1-91066715-6

e-pub ISBN 978-1-910667-16-3

mobi ISBN 978-1-910667-17-0

### SELF-HELP

### *Have You Seen My Ummm... Memory?*

An invaluable booklet for all whose memories are declining. Student memory tips as well as advice for those more senior moments to get through life.

ISBN 0-7552-0146-9

New Generation

ISBN American edition 978-1-4327-3364-3

Outskirts Press

*Ponderings* IN LARGE PRINT

Poems and short stories, as it says, in large print.

ISBN 0-7552-0169-8

New Generation Publishing.

## *It's Me, Honest It Is*

Commissioned by the NHS nursing service, this is an end-of-life handbook for individuals to complete.

## Coming in 2021

### *Love in Flanders Trenches*

A World War 1 saga of a nurse imprisoned as a suffragist and released to serve in the trenches, where she eventually finds love.

### *Dementia Adventure and Seaweed in my Hair*

The further adventures of Sgt. Rory Murdoch on the Isle of Arran.

# A BONUS STORY: THE DAY I CONFRONTED USAMA BIN LADEN

Our border collie, Tâche, died in the first few days of October 2005. I mention this for two reasons. Firstly that it made me temporarily depressed and I was not taking in the news every day. Secondly, I was no longer under a canine regime of regular walks. However, I was reminded about the dreadful earthquake of October 8th, 2005 by a friendly special police officer who ran a successful Indian restaurant in town. Farooq Ahmed lost his niece in this disaster and he told me he was going out to manage aid which was arriving in deluge proportions at Islamabad. He knew I had been the Regional Reporter to the Children's Hearings for Dumfries and Galloway and also knew I had retired recently. He asked if I would be willing to go to the NWFP of the Islamic Republic of Pakistan to assist in the care of the children in a large camp at Mundihar. With no dog and an unprotesting wife, I prepared to travel.

I arrived in Islamabad on 7th January 2006 with a case full of balloons, drawing books, exercise jotters, a few books, string, and my mouth organ which had to make an appearance at London Heathrow as well as Abbotabad's security. I was driven 130 kilometres into the NWFP to reach the Camp at Mundihar. The ground had been donated by a farmer and lay in tiered circles round a gentle hill. Twenty-four and a half thousand people lived in tents on this farmland which lacked hygiene, sufficient food, and warmth. On the second day I was called to a meeting. The atmosphere was tense. A brigadier of the Pakistani army chaired the meeting. The farmer's wife had been found donating aid to the townsfolk. It was a serious matter and the Brigadier made no bones about the situation. I raised my hand. The brigadier looked up and gave me his attention.

I spoke of world disasters and how people instinctively donated food, clothing, and money to aid charities. Such aid came flying out to where it is needed but there is often no administration on hand to deliver it. I saw this as a similar situation. What was needed was a responsible structure and rotas so everyone gets aid and knows when it is arriving.

The brigadier stood up and pointed at me. 'Sir, you are not a Muslim.' I acknowledged his statement with a nod. 'You are independent. I make you the camp manager,' and so my role changed dramatically. It became a 24/7 job with distribution of food and blankets a priority in the cold January weeks. There were feuds to resolve amid pointed Kalashnikovs but I kept mine in a safe place. Rain seeping down the terraces caused fury again when arms were the way to resolve dispute like the current knife crimes of London. Then I took ill.

I lost all energy and came down with an influenza type ailment. I was taken to a building to recover in Mansehra where underneath a banner, Muslim Hands Eye Clinic, I lay on a mattress semi-conscious. After two days I was beginning to feel better and sat up on my floor bedding and heard a car enter the compound. I heard two car doors close.

Being the only person available on the ground floor, I got up and went to the door. On the compound ground before me stood a very tall man. The tallest man I had seen in Pakistan by far. He was about my height, as I stood on the raised forecourt. He wore a cream chemise. His face was long with a straggly grey beard and piercing eyes. He looked very familiar. 'Salaam Alaikum' I said bringing my beard close to his cheek. 'Alaikum Salaam' he replied. There was a stand-off silence for a moment before he asked of someone of whom I had no knowledge.

'Then who are you?' he asked accusingly. 'I am the camp manager at Mundihar. I am recovering here from a cold.'

His eyes narrowed as he asked his final question. 'Where are you from?'

I told him 'Scotland' and on hearing this, without any further conversation, he turned and moved as quickly as his lame leg could travel back to the car with its engine running. It was a cotton blue four-seated car. It left the compound at speed and left me dazed as I saw it turn towards the town of Abbotabad. Yes, there was no doubt not only by his sudden departure but his stature and perfect English, I had met Usama bin Laden.

I returned to my mattress and saw my Kalashnikov. A thought ran through my head of having used it but the consequences could have been dire. There was much respect shown to Usama bin Laden locally as one who had stood up to the might of the USA. Furthermore, when I received some visitors that night I was told he often was seen around the shops in the town of 4 million people.

The date was Sunday 26th February 2006 and Usama had acquired his home in Abbotabad.

On my return to Scotland, I informed my member of parliament and the Chief Constable about the world's leading terrorist in Abbotabad but they thought I was wrong. Both told me he was hiding in an Afghan mountain retreat. I suspect they thought I was deluded.

On 2nd May 2011 Usama bin Laden paid the price. He was shot by US Seals and buried at sea under strict Islamic laws.

Vindicated at last, I told a few 'I told you so,' and they apologised. But an extra five years in constant fear of being discovered was an additional burden for Usama bin Laden to bear and I did not grudge him that.

*Miller Caldwell*

*My diary of my life in the Islamic Republic of Pakistan was published as **7 point 7 on the Richter Scale.***

Printed in Great Britain
by Amazon

63319617R00113